Hidden Treasures

Hidden Treasures

A novel

by

Paddi Newlin, K. R. Hartley, and Jessica Oliver

Cover art by Nikki Yannikos
Photo credit: R. S. Cilley

Chapter 1
The Diary

I knew the minute I laid eyes on the trunk in the antique store that I had to have it. It was gorgeous, a deep chocolate brown with sturdy black straps and beautiful brass locks. It reminded me of something straight out of *Titanic*. My mind immediately went to my Grandmother's handmade quilts and how they would be protected inside of it and still have a decorative piece for the house. I had been looking for the perfect thing to store them in for years and I knew that I had found it. I could feel there was something special about the trunk that magnetically drew me to it, almost as if it were begging me to take it home.

Ok, I'll admit it, a lot of things called out to me to take them home. That's why I had spotted the antique store in the first place. I dropped the kids off at school that morning and I couldn't bear to walk back into that mess of a house. I literally couldn't stand to be in that place one more minute. I had been aimlessly driving around since 8 am. The "stuff" in that house had completely taken over all our living spaces and if that's not enough, my entire mind. It was suffocating to even walk through the front door. My nerves were fried and I was at my wits end. That's when I found myself in front of the antique store.

I walked into the store and my eyes immediately fell on the amazing trunk. Gently I began to pull on its lid in an effort to open it, but it didn't budge an inch. I wasn't giving up. I could feel there was something special about this trunk and I HAD to know what it was. I pulled harder and harder, using all my strength, until suddenly the locks snapped open unexpectedly and I fell to the hard floor with a loud thud.

I couldn't wait to see what was inside. The lining was a horrible rotten looking shade of dark brown. Yuck! There were some crumpled papers and trash stuffed into the bottom of it but nothing that even remotely seemed special. I would have to get that cleaned out before I showed my husband my new treasure. I'm sure he would think it was just more junk, but I knew better.

My loud thud must have caught the attention of the store owner. Tall and rotund, with overalls and a five o'clock shadow (actually, it was probably closer to a 9 o'clock shadow), he walked down the aisle toward me and greeted me through his big toothy grin with, "Howdy ma'am! You ready to haggle for this thang?"

"Uhhhhh, sure," I replied, not really knowing what I was in for or what to think of this burly man.

Then my heart sank as I saw the price marked on the tag and realized it was way out of my range. It was too high to even try to begin negotiating. And besides, I was never very good at negotiating. So, I said thank you to the big burly man and began to walk away.

"Looks like I got myself a greenhorn!" his voice boomed from behind me.

The confused look on my face must have told him I didn't have a clue what he meant because he continued, "I mean you're new to this, aren't you?"

I turned on my heels, a bit startled by his loud laughter, then responded, "Well, yes but, it's way out of my price range so I didn't want to waste your time, or mine," I added.

2

He smiled, "Now where's the fun in that? We have to haggle in this business. If there were no bargaining involved, nobody would enjoy antiquing a'tall. If them fish hauled off and just jumped in yer boat, there wouldn't be no reason to throw those worms in the water right? And that's half the fun."

I smiled back, "I see your point, but I'm afraid I'm just not very good at fishing...errrr, I mean negotiating."

He looked at me thoughtfully, then after a few seconds of awkward silence he said with a slight crack in his voice, "My wife was the same way. She never could negotiate a price. She just passed away a few years ago. You sure do remind me a lot of her in her younger days." Sticking out his hand to shake mine he said, "The name's Fred. Nice to meet ya, Greenhorn."

Smiling, I replied, "You can call me Courtney".

"Ok, Miss Courtney, how 'bout this; you make me an offer and we'll go from there."

I took a deep breath and thought to myself, "This is going to be embarrassing, but..." I began to pull out all the wadded up bills I had stuffed into my purse and placed them into Fred's big hands. I knew it wasn't going to be nearly enough to cover that beautiful trunk. But, as I took the last crumpled dollar bill out of the bottom of my purse, Fred stopped me and said, "Greenhorn! You got yerself a deal!" I couldn't believe it. I couldn't possibly have given him even half of what the trunk was worth. He was right, this negotiating.... I mean fishing.... I mean negotiating WAS fun!

After filling out some paperwork and handing me my receipt, the trunk was officially mine. Once it was loaded in my car, Fred shook my hand and said, "Now don't you be a stranger, Miss

Courtney. Come back anytime for another fishing lesson." As I walked away, I heard him mutter to himself, "She always said when the time came, I'd know who to give it to. She was right. As usual." I wasn't quite sure what he meant by that but before I could ask, the door to the shop had swung shut and Fred was nowhere to be seen.

I have to say it: I was feeling pretty proud of myself for learning to haggle and leaving with my bargain. I smiled to myself the whole way home thinking of all the things I could use my new trunk for. It felt more like a treasure than a second-hand trunk thanks to Fred.

Fast-forward two months: I had to buy some new laundry hampers. Those plastic ones break so easily, especially when they're weighted down with 40 pounds of clothes. I picked them up at the store and realized when I went to load them in the car that my prized trunk was still in the back of my SUV! How could I have forgotten it was in there?

Oh my goodness! Speaking of forgetting important things! I had forgotten my perfectionist mother-in-law was coming into town tomorrow, and my car was a complete disaster! I wouldn't dare let her see my car like this! Especially when hers is the epitome of clean. And by clean, I mean the white glove kind of clean. I crammed the hampers in the back seat and hurried home to get all the junk out of my car.

When I opened the rear hatch of the car, everything came flying out onto the driveway. Who knew this junk was spring loaded? McDonald's wrappers and not quite empty cups scattered all around me and the trunk bounced out at my feet. I barely had time to move my foot out of the way. A split second later and my toes would have been crushed. AGAIN! You'd think after the last trip to the ER, I'd have learned not to wear flip flops.

4

I glanced inside my once gorgeous trunk and saw all the trash and papers I had forgotten were shoved in the bottom of it. I looked up and saw the trash can up against the house in the driveway and thought, "This may be as close as I get to the trash can this week. Better take advantage of it before the mother-in-law gets here!" I began cleaning out the garbage and pulling out all those papers. I remember wondering if the people who sold it knew they had left so many things inside? From what I could tell, it was mostly unimportant stuff: notes from school, a few coloring books, some loose leaf papers with lists written on them, magazine articles about a character called "The FlyLady," a pink covered paperback book called <u>Sink Reflections,</u> and some pictures cut out of a magazine and taped on to some of the papers. "Why would anyone save all this?" It just looked like junk to me.

As I pulled out the magazines and book, something gold caught my eye. There, tucked away in a side pocket was a beautiful book. It was brown leather bound with gold trimmed pages and tied with a purple satin bow around the middle. There was a small note attached to the ribbon that simply read: "This diary is meant for someone special. You are special."

I was very careful not to harm the pages as I opened the cover. The first page was blank except for these words:

"To Find Joy in All That I Do"

Hmm. No name, just some very intriguing words. My interest was piqued.

I began to read the diary from the beginning:

Dear Diary,

Today was just a bad day. It actually started last night. As I was getting into bed, Ethan informed me that his project for English was due tomorrow. Project? What project? He had forgotten to tell me. Or maybe he had told me and I was the one that had forgotten. That didn't matter now. Either way, it wasn't done. I scrambled to locate some poster board and pictures and interesting stories... at 11:00 PM, no less. I pulled every magazine from whatever chair, desk, and pile I could find. Why do my children ALWAYS wait until the last minute for this stuff?? A flood of guilt came over me as I realized that they learned it from me. Procrastination was my middle name. But there was no time to worry about that now. After lots of searching, Ethan and I were able to cut some pictures out of the magazines for the posters and were ready to glue them on but.... where was that glue stick?

I racked my brain to remember where the glue stick was. Oh, wait, I know! Probably in the kid's room who had the last project due. Yep. After searching and searching, I found it right there stuck to the floor in Karly's room where I had left it. I pried it loose from the floor and returned to Ethan's room to help him finish. I was greeted by the soft sound of snoring. During my frantic searching, he had fallen fast asleep. And what kid wouldn't? It was well after midnight by now. I began to glue and got it all done by 1:00 AM. Not terrible. I've done worse.

The alarm buzzed at 6:00 AM. Yeah right! Snooze.

I awoke to Ethan telling me a picture had fallen off the poster. Could I please fix it? Sure. I glued it back on only to look at the clock. 7:35? No way! So much for the snooze button! I threw on the first thing I saw: a pair of old baggy sweatpants, a T-shirt full of holes and "proudly" displaying Tweety Bird, and the fluffy pink bunny slippers the kids had given me for Mother's Day last year, and frantically began throwing everything in the car: book bags, homework and kids.

I went flying down the street. That's when all three kids started complaining, "Mom! We're hungry!!!" Oops! McDonald's it is… again. I should own stock by now. Just my luck. The drive thru was packed and I didn't have time to wait. I had no choice and ran inside where there was no line. Evelyn took the order. (Yes, I'm pretty much on a first name basis with everyone there.) I got the food, threw it in the back seat, and sped toward the school, not slowing down until I saw the blinking lights of the school zone. I guess I slowed down a little too fast because suddenly I was wearing my coffee all over my white sweatpants. The kids exited quickly and slammed the door behind them without even a goodbye to me. I couldn't understand why. I had gotten them dressed, fed and at school on time.

Ethan's project: Check.
Breakfast: Check.
Kids at school on time: Check.

It was about this time that I noticed the car beginning to sputter and jerk. Not again! What else can possibly go wrong? I was SO mad at Dan. He told me he was going to take it to the shop and get it fixed. How could he let me drive this death trap? It finally sputtered to a stop and died. I managed to get it pulled off to the shoulder of the road and out of traffic. I was livid. I didn't care if Dan was in a meeting with the president of the company, I was going to call him and let him have it. I was going to give him a piece of my mind. Tell him exactly how I felt. What kind of a man would let his wife drive around in a pile of junk like this?

Ok, maybe not. My cell phone was dead.

7

I tried to start the clunker again. Lots of noise. No results. Just as I slammed my fist onto the steering wheel, I looked up and saw none other than Debbie; my nosy neighbor. Of course she's wearing her size 6 designer dress, 5-inch stiletto heels, perfect hair and flawlessly applied makeup. And I'm wearing fluffy bunny slippers. I looked like a cartoon character. Just like Tweety Bird on my shirt. Oh, my goodness! I forgot about that stupid bird on my shirt! Let the embarrassment begin. There wasn't enough time to duck so I just rolled down the window.

"Hey, darlin'. Are you ok?" Debbie whined in her nasally voice.

"Actually, the car is broken down. Can I borrow your cell phone, Debbie?"

"Well, of course you can," she drawled with that sickeningly sweet but fake sounding Southern accent. Everybody knew she was from Wisconsin.

I dialed Dan's number. Boy, was he going to get it. He finally answered, "Hello?"

"You forgot to fix the car, Dan! I'm stranded here!"

"But I did fix it."

"Well, if it was fixed then WHY am I stranded here on the side of the road?"

That's about the time Debbie, with her head stuck halfway in the driver's window, commented, "Oh, honey. I see your problem. You're out of gas!"

Really? Of course I am. I completely forgot about the dinging sound and the large yellow flashing light on my dashboard during my rush to get the kids off to school. I suppose the only fortunate part of this was that I was in front of a gas station.

It was probably the combination of Debbie's whiny voice and the fact that her head was sticking inside my window causing me to lean toward the passenger seat, but her announcement about my gas gauge was easily heard through the cell phone. Dan calmly replied, "Next time watch the gauge. 'E' stands for 'empty.' That's automobile 101. Oh, and by the way, Ethan's school called. They can't get a hold of you. Let me guess: Your cell phone's dead AGAIN? Ethan left his project in the car." And with that, he hung up with a loud click in my ear.

I glanced over my shoulder to see the poster on the floor, among the French fries, paper cups, and socks. I pulled it out and set it in front of me... right in the coffee.

It was about here that Debbie commented, "Shout."

Not that I didn't feel like it. But, why in the world was she telling me to shout? Debbie, Little Miss Perfect, would never be caught dead shouting but she wants me to? I must have had a dumbfounded look on my face because then she continued, "Shout will take that coffee stain right out of those pants. Why, honey, they'll be just like new again."

I handed the phone back to her... so I wouldn't throw it. I managed to squeeze out a thank you through my gritted teeth, all the while wondering how quickly the rest of the neighbors would hear about this.

I walked toward the gas station and as I looked at Debbie I watched her gleefully punching buttons on her cell phone knowing that I was about to become the latest, juiciest piece of gossip in town. I fought back the tears that were stinging my eyes.

The attendant was nice enough to help me get enough gas in the car to start it, drive it to the pump and fill it up. After making the trip back to Ethan's school, I took his poster inside. I was so embarrassed, but not nearly as much as Ethan, as he and his friends from the playground watched me entering the school in those awful slippers and coffee stained sweatpants. And not to mention that my hair looked like it had a rat's nest in it. I'd never gotten the chance to brush it this morning with all the rushing around we did. But what could I do? I ran in, dropped it off, and as I was leaving I was sure that Ethan's friends were giving him a hard time about me. To help him save face, I didn't wave or even glance in his direction. Maybe he could pretend I was somebody else's mom. He ducked his head and walked away.

As I pulled back into the driveway, I saw Debbie and the other three ladies from the neighborhood laughing and chattering. Funny. They stopped talking as soon as they saw my car. I knew that wouldn't take long.

To make matters worse, I walked into my house, slamming the door behind me, thinking when would I be able to finally call this a home? The clutter closed in on me everywhere I looked, making me feel like a claustrophobic person in an airplane bathroom. I walked from the garage and into the kitchen. Ugh.... the kitchen. A mountain of dirty dishes poured out of the sink covering the counters, tables, and floors. I just couldn't deal with it. So I thought, "I'll go in the living room and turn on the television," only to be greeted by a monstrous mound of laundry. Clean clothes but unfolded. Or were they clean? I couldn't remember. I picked them up only to find soggy paper plates crusted and stained with some long forgotten dinner from who knows when. I picked up the plates realizing only then that they were actually stuck to

10

the clothes. That answered my earlier question. The clothes were definitely dirty.

After being on the floor they were covered with cat hair anyway. I couldn't remember the last time I vacuumed. I guess you have to be able to see the floor and have some idea where you left the vacuum to do that. I glanced around at the sewing, magazines, and stuff that represented countless projects I had started and hadn't finished.

I climbed over the toys and trash in the hallway to retreat to my bedroom only to hear the doorbell ring. I didn't care who it was. There was no way I was going to answer that door. I sat down in the midst of the trash too overwhelmed to move.

Why does everybody else have their life together? Why do their houses look so good? How do they have time to get everything all together and I can't even get out of these bunny slippers? It can't be that hard! If everybody else can do it, why can't I? What's wrong with me?

Something has to change. Something HAS to change.

I stopped reading the diary for a moment to grab a glass of tea. As I did, I was thinking: this lady in the diary could understand my life. I curled up in the chair and continued reading the diary...

Chapter 2
Tomorrow Never Comes, But I'm Still Waiting

Dear Diary,

Something has to change. I know it does. I'm pretty desperate, but I'm not sure what to do. Where do I start?

I really don't like change. But I don't like where I am right now even more.

I've been a lot like Scarlett O'Hara in Gone with the Wind. Like Scarlett, I normally liked to think about things "tomorrow." That's been my motto: "I'll start on that tomorrow." Unfortunately tomorrow never gets here. Well, I'm done with that. Today is the day. No more tomorrows. Only today.

I needed to know where to start so, I Googled it. I wasn't even sure what to search. I just decided to put in how I was feeling. I just can't process all these feelings! I'm so... overwhelmed.

"Overwhelmed." That was definitely how I felt. What else? What else?

Good grief! I can't even organize my thoughts! "Disorganized." There's another one.

But does that really sum it up? Let me see. Disorganized definitely applies, but it's deeper than that. It's like everything in my life is messed up. It's complete chaos. Yes. "Chaos." That sums it all up.

I'll just put in all three and see what happens. "Overwhelmed, Discouraged, Chaos." Seeing those three words in the search

13

engine for some weird reason made me smile. Maybe there was something in me telling me an answer might be on the way.

I hit enter.

The first entry was <u>Sink Reflections</u> by somebody called "The FlyLady."

<u>Sink Reflections</u> by the FlyLady? Wasn't that the book that was in my new trunk? I would have to check that out, but I didn't want to stop reading the diary. Where was I? Oh, yes...

...somebody called "The FlyLady." "The FlyLady"? Really?? I need help with my life, not pest control!

I clicked on the link anyway. It's a book. No, wait. It's a person, a radio show, a magazine, a website... WHAT IS THIS? It's supposed to help organize a life filled with chaos. There was that word: CHAOS!

The book seemed to be a good starting point. I thought about ordering the book, but instead I went to the bookstore so I could get started right away. I bought it, came home, and started reading immediately.

From the very beginning, the book related to exactly where I was. I couldn't put it down. The more I read, the more it sounded like it was written about me.

I read and read. And before I knew it, I was turning the last page.

2:55 PM! Oh no! I was late to pick up the kids. I pulled up to the school and naturally they were the last ones standing there. The teachers were giving me dirty looks. It doesn't really matter, since they already think I'm the worst mother anyway. This Tweety Bird sweatshirt wasn't helping my reputation much either.

Oh, good grief! Here came Ethan's teacher, dragging him by the hand.

Oh, my goodness! He had a black eye!! Are you kidding me? What had happened to my baby?

I jumped out of the car and ran to Ethan asking, "Are you ok?"

Before he could even answer, the teacher interrupted him by saying; "He got in a little tiff with one of the other kids."

"Ethan!" I scolded, "What in the world did you get in a fight for??"

Lowering his head in shame, he replied, "One of the other boys was making fun of the way you looked, Mommy, so I hit him."

I sheepishly thanked the teacher and pulled Ethan into the car. Brittany, my teenage daughter, immediately jumped on me, "What do you expect, Mom? You can't look like that in front of our friends! It's embarrassing! I'm surprised he doesn't get beat up every day, the way you look!"

I shot a look to the back seat at Brittany. She rolled her eyes but at least she quit talking.

Ethan, ever the defender, looked at Brittany and said, "My Mommy is beautiful!"

The silence in the car was deafening on the way home. Brittany was right. Sometimes I think the kids would be better off without me. But I can do better. I will do better! I have to make things better. My thoughts drifted back to the FlyLady book. Maybe there is hope.

What did she say to do? Where did she say to start? Oh, oh! Now I remember. Shine my sink. Shine my sink? With this kind of chaos, I am supposed to shine my sink??

It sounded crazy. I didn't see how that's going to help, but I've tried it my way and it hadn't worked. It was time to try something else. After I got everybody to bed, I went to the kitchen sink that was filled with mystery water. First I had to reach into the filth that I had let accumulate and pull everything out. Ok, I didn't quite reach in. I grabbed the tongs from the grill, held my nose and dove into the mystery water. So there was that plate I had been looking for! It was underneath a Barbie doll and what I'm pretty sure was a chunk of silly putty. Why were they in there? Who knows? But that wasn't my task right now.

I pulled out some cleaning materials and realized I had absolutely no place to put them. I suppose I would have to clean the counters first. I remembered, FlyLady said, "Get a box." My house was full of boxes, none of which were empty of course. So I found the box that had the least amount of stuff in it and dumped everything on the dining room floor. Then I noticed the Rubbermaid tub sitting beside the chair. It was my favorite color. I emptied it out, too, and used that instead.

I would describe my counter, but there were so many things on it, I wouldn't know where to begin. Let's just call it "stuff" and leave it at that. Two items to note: the electric bill from two months ago that I didn't pay and I accused them of never sending to me when our power got cut off and my son's report card that I was supposed to sign and send back that I had accused him of losing. I couldn't be bothered with those details right now though. I was on a mission.

So I took my arm and scooped everything into the tub and put my cleaning products on the counter.

I swear: I have EVERY cleaning product known to man! I thought that if I had the "perfect" product, that it would get my house clean. The problem is... you actually have to _use_ them for things to get clean. They don't just clean themselves no matter what that infomercial says! I suddenly remembered that FlyLady's book had detailed cleaning instructions on how to shine your sink, so I went back to find it... page 3. There it was: Point by point. I saw that I didn't need all those cleaning products. She said I could just use hot water and bleach on certain sinks. Thank goodness mine was one of them! So, I tossed all the cleaning items into the tub and got out a scrub brush (ok, it was actually an old toothbrush) and I scrubbed the handles and the faucets and places around the sides (you know, the place where the sink actually fits into the hole in the counter).

Interesting fact: If you use that white stuff to seal your sink (caulking I think it's called) and you don't clean it, it actually turns black... who knew?? I thought it was some sort of decorative paint finish; come to find out it's actually mold.

And so, I cleaned my sink. After scrubbing and cleaning every crevice, I did it again. I'll be honest: I didn't really know when to quit. 1:23 AM. I guess that's time to quit. I sat down on the floor, exhausted; next to the blue tub overflowing with clutter, wondering what good it was going to do to clean my sink with all this clutter surrounding me.

Oh well, it was time to head to bed anyway. Tomorrow morning was going to come awfully early. I turned off all the lights except one small light in case anyone got up for a drink of water during the night. As I walked out of the room, something caught my eye— a glimmer. I turned to see what it was. It was that sink. It was

17

actually sparkling; shining in the almost darkened room. I stopped and gazed at what I had done. Tears began to spill from my eyes and drop onto my cheeks. That sink shined back at me and I could see my own reflection as I wiped my tears away. That sink, MY sink, as weird as it might seem… was my glimmer of hope.

It may not seem like much to others, but it was a step in the right direction. FlyLady said if I could take just one step in the right direction they would begin to add up. I took that first step today.

Sink clean: Check.

Chapter 3
Baby Step 2: Before Bedtime Routine

Dear Diary,

I sit here at the end of a very exhausting day. I have worked SO hard, but I barely made a dent in this mess.

I feel so worthless. I know Dan thinks I'm lazy and I sit around the house all day watching soap operas and eating Fritos, but that's NOT the truth! I work my rear off all day! He just can't see it. Ok, to be honest, neither can I.

Every time I look at this cluttered house, all I can hear is the voice of my mother, "Why can't you do ANYTHING right? No man will ever want a woman who is this sloppy and lazy!" I wish I could get those words out of my head.

Maybe I should just explain everything that happened today.

The day started off in a weird way. Do you ever have that feeling at night that somebody is watching you? That's exactly the feeling I had at 5:30 this morning. I opened my eyes to see Karly standing two inches from my face, staring at me, and then saying, "Mommy! I had a bad dream. I'm scared. Can I get in bed with you??" That's normal at our house. I let her climb into bed with me. About 20 minutes later I realized Karly (also known to me as the human helicopter) wasn't going to let me sleep anymore as I was hit with a flurry of elbows, knees and feet.

I finally surrendered my bed to her and climbed out. Less than four hours of sleep. I knew this would be a long day. I walked downstairs to the mess that is my house. I knew I had a lot to do, but I hadn't a clue where to start. I started working on picking up anything I could find.

19

Before I knew it, Ethan came thundering down the stairs around 7:00 AM. He was yelling something about pancakes, but I wasn't in the mood to fix anything. I told him to get a donut. That's when I heard him calling from the kitchen, "Hey, Mom! What are all these bottles in the big tub for?"

Oh my gosh! I had left all that cleaning stuff on the kitchen floor in that tub! I ran into the kitchen, yanked the bottle out of Ethan's hands and screamed, "Don't touch that! That's dangerous!" Ethan innocently replied, "Then what's it doing on the floor?" From the mouths of babes...

I found a shelf in the pantry where the tub could fit and I stuck it up as high as I could on the shelf. I looked at the kitchen (which was a wreck) but in the middle of the mess was a sparkling sink smiling at me. Without thinking, I found myself smiling back at it.

Dan was the next one downstairs. Half-dressed, he was muttering about not having any clean socks. Would it kill a husband to get his own socks?? I wasn't going to get in another argument with him. I was still hurt over the last one.

I can still hear his words ringing in my ears. How could I forget them? He said them so often, they constantly ring in my ears.

"Why don't you take care of yourself and our home? What's wrong with you?

"You've let yourself go! When we got married you were so beautiful. It's like you don't even care anymore. You never fix yourself up for me. You always wear those frumpy stained sweats and an old T-shirt with holes in it. Haven't you ever wondered why when we go to bed at night I always face away from you?? I can barely stand to look at you! Don't you want me to be proud of you?

I'm ashamed to take you anywhere because of how you look. People think I can't afford to buy you nice things. It looks like I spend all my money on me. Why are you wearing that JUNK? Do you not even care about me anymore?

"And this house is a pigsty! If Child Services saw this place, they'd take our kids away! Seriously! WHAT DO YOU DO ALL DAY??? Sit around and watch TV? I'm at the office all day working to support this family so you can stay home and do NOTHING?"

I just burst into tears. He looked at me, stormed out and slammed the door.

It's not like I don't try. I just don't have enough time and nobody in this household lifts a finger to help me with anything! It's like I'm just here to be their cook and their maid! If he only knew how hard I work and he never gives me credit for ANYTHING. I snapped back to today.

I watched Dan pull two socks out of the pile of clothes on the kitchen table. I tried to be cheery and said, "Good morning!" but as he looked at me and said, "Good morning," the look on his face said everything. His eyes scanned me up and down, looking at me from head to toe. The look of disgust that followed spoke more than any words he could've said.

He stopped to pat Ethan on the head and said, "Morning, champ."

"Hey, Dad!"

Then, Dan tripped over some junk on the floor. I thought he was going to comment on it, but instead he shook his head and said, "I don't know why I'm even asking this, but did you remember to pick up my dry cleaning yesterday?"

21

He told me to do that yesterday! WHY did I always forget? I am such an AIRHEAD! There were my mother's words in my face, strong and loud, "No man will want a sloppy, lazy woman." It was a wonder he hadn't left me already.

Trying to smile, I replied, "I'll go get it for you right now. I'm sorry."

With the deepest sarcasm a person could muster, he replied, "No. No. I don't want to interrupt your 'busy' schedule. I'm sure you won't have time. I'll get it myself." He went back upstairs, shaking his head and mumbling something under his breath. I felt like the wind had been knocked out of me.

Brittany came downstairs at 7:30. She was dressed, hair fixed, school bag in hand. She was so organized. It was like she was my mother reborn. She was 15, but I swear she was born 40. She always seemed to have everything together. She walked into the kitchen, tripped over the same stuff Dan did, rolled her eyes, then blurted out in an irritated tone, "Is there anything for breakfast?"

I only had 15 more minutes to get the other two ready. I knew there was no way I could fix her anything. But I offered anyway, "Pop Tarts, toast or a donut."

Another roll of the eyes, as only a teenager can do...

"Look! I have to get Karly ready for school. I don't have time to fix anything now. Come downstairs earlier and I'll have enough time to fix you some breakfast."

"Mom! You act like us eating breakfast every morning is a surprise. This is ridiculous! We NEVER eat a real breakfast. I could get down here at 5 and there still wouldn't be anything!

Brooke's house is NEVER like this! They always eat together. And their house isn't a garbage dump like ours is either! I'm too embarrassed to ever invite my friends over here! WHY DO WE HAVE TO LIVE LIKE THIS?" And with that stinging remark, she yanked the last donut from the box, walked into the garage, slamming the door, but not before I heard her say, "I HATE DONUTS!"

After an awkward pause, Ethan shook his head saying, "Man. That girl has issues!"

"What's issues?" asked Karly.

I interrupted, "Both of you, go up to your room and get your clothes out." They both scampered upstairs.

I wanted to cry. Brittany had no business talking to me like that, but everything she said was right. It was like hearing my mother all over again through my child's voice. It hurt. I am such a failure. Why is it every other person on the planet has their act together and I don't? Was I just born with the inability to organize anything?

As I was thinking all this, Ethan came around the corner in his jeans with no socks and no shirt. Dan was right behind him. He was fully dressed in his suit and picking up his briefcase.

I pointed my finger at Ethan and said, "I told you to get ready!"

"I'm sorry, Mom! I can't find my socks or a clean shirt!"

Dan chimed in, "Just check the pile on the table, Champ. That's where just about everything is in this house." It was my time to roll my eyes.

23

Dan called to Brittany, "Come on, Brittany, I'll take you to school. Your brother and sister will be a while."

Ethan glibly replied, "Psycho sister is in the garage pouting."

Dan thumped him on the head and said, "Don't talk about your sister that way. She's just frustrated right now," and as he looked at me walking out the door he added, "Like a LOT of us."

As Dan was shutting the door, I heard Brittany reply, "Good! At least I won't be late and my friends won't have to see Mom's sweatpants. Thank you, Daddy!"

Trying to hide my sadness, I said, "Here, Nathan, let me get it for you. I reached to the bottom of the mass of unfolded clothes (At least I generally knew where they were!) and found his socks. I tossed them to him.

"Mom! These don't match!" he whined.

I turned back to him and yelled, "JUST PUT THEM ON!"

His eyes were as wide as mine. I think I was just as shocked that I had said it, but my frustration point was pressing me beyond what I could control. He left the room to finish putting on his clothes. I had just wounded my only defender and we both knew it. His slumped shoulders and shuffling feet told me there was a very sad little boy walking away from me.

Karly walked in wearing an orange top with pink pants, black socks, green shoes, and a bright yellow bow clipped crookedly in her hair. She looked like a mixed up Baby Gap holiday mannequin, but there wasn't time for her to change. I still didn't have their book bags ready.

I told her to get in the car. I grabbed my keys and yelled for Ethan to come on. He came around the corner, head down, still upset from me yelling at him. He didn't say a word during the entire trip to school. As I dropped him off, I waved goodbye to a puffy eyed, teary faced boy who was quite possibly my biggest fan. What was wrong with me? I couldn't think about that because Karly was talking my head off all the way to her school. That's probably just as well. I didn't need to talk at that moment. We made it to the school and Karly got out of the car in her "fabulous" outfit. The teacher who helps with the car line just looked at her, then looked at me like I was crazy.

I sheepishly tried to explain, "She wanted to dress herself this morning."

Karly immediately turned and reported, "This was all that was left. Everything else was dirty."

Now the entire faculty at Eastside Elementary knew my awful truth.

I wanted to scream, "YES! THAT'S RIGHT! I'm a TERRIBLE MOTHER!" Then I figured, why state the obvious? Every parent who just saw my kid already knew it. The teacher looked at Karly not quite knowing what to say, then looked back at me in the car, still in my wonderful morning outfit with flip-flops and a ball cap pulled over my head, and awkwardly said, "Have a nice day."

On the drive back home, I was thinking, "I'm going to get a lot done today. I'm going to change this! If I want it bad enough, I can conquer this!"

I was full of motivation, ready to begin, but as I looked at the piles and piles of junk I honestly didn't know where to start! I noticed Ethan had tossed a plate and glass into my sink!! Could he not see that it was already clean?? All I had to do was wipe it out though. It was easy since I had just shined it. I put the dishes in the dishwasher and wiped out the sink. It was pretty and shiny all over again. No harm done.

It had taken me years to get into this mess. FlyLady said it took her nine months to get her routine down. Routine? I really had no routine. The only consistency in my life was going from crisis to crisis and I was tired of it. If only I knew where to begin, then I could make some progress.

I decided to start by rearranging one bedroom. Who knows? It might even make Dan happier. So I spent all day working on it. Before I knew it, it was time to pick up the kids. I surveyed the bedroom and honestly, it still looked awful. All I had done was move the clutter to a different place in the room.

Once again, another WASTED day. Now I had the kids at home from school. I got so busy organizing the bedroom that I had nothing for dinner thawed out. So... pizza again. Ethan and Karly would be happy, but Dan would be furious. I knew he would be livid with me for my lack of accomplishment and that I had wasted more money on fast food.

Dread filled me on the inside knowing I had another fight with Dan right around the corner. I knew he was going to be home any minute. Maybe if I called him it would soften the blow. At least if he was going to yell it would be over the phone and the kids wouldn't have to pretend they didn't hear it again.

I asked Brittany if she had seen my cell phone. She sarcastically replied, "Who knows? If you're calling Dad, he's working late and won't be home for supper... as if he wants pizza anyway."

I thought to myself, "Nice of him to tell his daughter and not his wife."

As Brittany pulled some fruit from the refrigerator (her supper), she continued, "And by the way, don't worry; I've already put everybody's clothes in the washer. Dad asked me to take care of the laundry."

Brittany looked me dead in the eye, with her hands on her hips, as she continued with the bobbing of her head that only a teenager can do, "__WE'VE__ decided __WE__ don't want to live like this any longer and so __WE'RE__ going to make some changes so __WE__ don't have to live in this garbage dump anymore. Dad came up with some ideas to fix all this and this is one of them."

I was stunned. "__WE'VE__ decided?" Who is "__WE__?" I was thinking.

Brittany served the kids their pizza, changed the clothes to the dryer and then ironed her Daddy's shirts. Then she put the kids to bed. As I watched all this occurring in my house, my overwhelming thought was, "Why was I even here?" They honestly don't need me. My child has now taken over the role of the adult in this family. I'm SO ashamed.

In the silence, downstairs, in the mess, through my tears I came to a point of desperation. I needed to do better for my family. I HAD to do better for my family. I love them. And because of them I HAD to change. I needed a routine. Then I remembered the FlyLady book. There was hope. Just like all those cleaners I had bought and didn't use, I had read the book and not followed through on her plan. I had to follow it for it to work.

I just had that book this morning. I couldn't remember where I had put it! I read it in the living room. After turning the living room upside down I thought maybe I had left it in the kitchen. So I went through cabinets, countertops… I even looked in the dishwasher. I couldn't find it! I looked through the books on the bookshelf in the living room, too. (As if I would actually put a book away!) As I searched the books, I accidentally dumped some of them on the floor. They were Dan's books, so I carefully put them back. But they kept falling over! So I found a couple of decorative bookends I had also purchased at an antique shop and propped them up on both sides so they would stay there.

I had spent all day in the bedroom; maybe I put it there. Nothing doing. It wasn't there either. I was going to have to run to the bookstore and buy another one. I thought, "I'll get a quick snack before I leave. I enjoyed those midmorning snacks. That's when I found it. The book was in the cheese tray at the bottom of the refrigerator. I don't have a clue how it got there, but I quit asking questions like that a long time ago.

I opened it up to where the FlyLady was talking about routines. It made so much sense to me. If I could just create a routine for my evenings, my mornings would go SO much smoother. I remembered Dan's books and the decorative bookends. The books stayed on the shelf when I used the bookends to prop them up. That's exactly what FlyLady was saying my day needed! Bookends! A before bedtime and morning routine would be my "bookends."

But what was this about dressing to my lace up shoes? According to the book I had to do that before I could begin.

FlyLady said that I needed to get up every morning and fix my face and put on shoes that lace up. She said it would make me feel more prepared for work. I wasn't sure how that worked, but I was willing to give it a try even if I hated wearing shoes in the house.

The book also said that I needed a bedtime routine that would prepare me for the next day. I needed to keep it very simple: Four *things or less. I picked up a pen from the floor in the living room and tore the back off an envelope, which was in a stack on the coffee table and I scribbled four things on the paper.*

Before Bedtime Routine

1.   *Check my schedule for the next day. I don't really have a calendar like some people do, but maybe I could pick one up tomorrow. I remembered a few details about Ethan's school trip. He would have to have $5. Karly needed her lunch money, too. I normally scrambled through my purse to find it every day or ran by the bank to get it on the way to school. I would be ahead of the game tomorrow. I would be prepared.*

2.   *Lay out my clothes for the next day including lace up shoes. FlyLady said I also needed to get the kids to lay out their clothes. I took Karly's clothes upstairs and told the older kids to lay out theirs also. They looked at me funny, but they did it.*

3.   *Put things needed for the next day by the door. I found the kids' book bags and set them next to the garage door. This area was going to become our "Launch Pad" as FlyLady called it. I set everything there. I put the money in Karly and Ethan's book bags.*

4.   *Me Time: I would take some quiet time just for myself. That's when I wrote all this. And I am happy to report that I am about to get into a hot bubble bath and enjoy some time for ME.*

I'm not sure how tomorrow will go, but I will sleep better tonight knowing I'm a little bit more prepared for it.

Chapter 4
The Little Engine

Dear Diary,

I know it's been three weeks since I last wrote but I've been working really hard on getting on this FlyLady Band Wagon. I misplaced you during the process. You know, I've never been one to write in a diary, but I actually missed writing. Somehow writing it down seems to help it all make sense. I'm not really sure if I can explain it, but it helps me to clear my mind and keep track of what's going on in my life. I'm working so hard all day that I seem to lose track of what I've actually done. Enough of that. I need to fill you in on what's been going on.

The first morning, after I had done my before bedtime routine and had my morning routine all planned out, was wonderful. I had written down a few simple steps to help keep me on track. When I started to get ready for bed I set a timer per FlyLady. The timer went off and I had everyone go check their school schedule for what they had to do the next day, sports gear needed, test papers signed, you know, all those things I wish I had somewhere on one calendar so I could see what was going on and when. To tell you the truth there was a lot of complaining and eye rolling but I stood my ground and got it done. There were a few glitches that I hadn't been prepared for. I failed to finish the laundry and a ball uniform needed to be washed before I could go to bed. But, at least it got done and in a sports bag before midnight. I sent everyone off to bed at a decent hour (except me). For the first time in a long time, I got my clothes laid out, and even washed my face and brushed my teeth before going to bed. It felt great!

Each day I learned something new about my before bedtime routine. I always included wiping down my sink and laying out a clean dishtowel. It's such a nice thing to be greeted by my gleaming

31

sink and a sweet smelling dishtowel rather than a moldy, stinky one and a sink full of filthy dishes. I've been going along each day with my new routines and the kids are starting to get the hang of it too. They even commented that they haven't had any more of those scary moments when they wondered if they had the papers they needed when it was time for school trips or returned papers from home. That was pretty amazing to hear.

But then, last night Dan and I had a disagreement… Ok, it was a huge argument right in front of the kids. I'm working so hard and all he does is find fault with me in everything I do. I couldn't take it anymore and went to bed and covered my head with the blankets to hide from it all. I didn't even do my before bedtime routine. This morning was a disaster of course, and to make it worse the kids are furious with me. They said I was running their Daddy away. The morning kept going downhill from there.

I had a note in my sink telling the family NOT to put their dishes in the sink in hopes that they would actually find the dishwasher where dirty dishes belong. Karly and Ethan thought it was funny, but Brittany just got irritated with me.

"Really, Mom? REALLY? It's bad enough to have this CRAP all over the house, but now we have to look at notes in our sink telling us what to do, too? Like one dirty dish in the sink is gonna make this house look any worse?"

It was hard, but I calmly told her to please be patient with me. I was making some changes around the house that are going to help everyone.

She just rolled her eyes, shook her head and said, "This is JUST like everything else you try. You start big and quit. I give it two weeks. Tops."

Her words stung. Why did she always have to be so negative? It hurt though, because deep down, I knew she was right. I had so many self-help books and boxes lying around the house, most of which were unopened, that I couldn't argue with her. I hoped with all my heart that this time would be different.

Everyone got off for school on time for once. Before leaving, Ethan looked in his lunchbox and smiled at me, "Mom! You remembered my chips! Awesome!" It made me feel a little better. At least I did one thing right this morning.

Maybe Dan was right last night. The house was still a mess. I thought to myself, somehow I'm going to MAKE this work. I figured I might as well start with the living room. I dove in. I worked hard all day. And as I looked at everything, it was just like my bedroom. It didn't seem like I had accomplished anything. All I had really done was move clutter from one pile to another. I had organized a pile of junk, but when it came down to it, it still looked like a pile of junk—just in a different place.

Then I remembered something FlyLady said, "**YOU CAN'T ORGANIZE CLUTTER!**" That is exactly what I had been doing. But what else could I do? It's not like I could just throw this stuff away!

After a day of working in the living room and getting nowhere, I thought that maybe I could clean something else before the end of the day but there was no way I could do it and do it right. I know this sounds stupid, but I was so overwhelmed that I started to cry, and that made me feel even worse. I knew that I had to do something that was positive. Wait…. Where did that thought come from? Then I realized: The FlyLady!

I decided to re-read her chapter on clutter to help me understand what to do with all of my junk. She gave a lot of her stuff away but

I just didn't know if I could do that. Dan's hard earned money had paid for all this stuff. How many times had I heard that phrase before? I began to look around the room and add up in my head just how much money I had spent on things we didn't really need.

It was time for me to take the plunge of de-cluttering and as luck would have it, I was out of garbage bags. I decided to drive to the store and pick some up. As I was walking out to my car, my neighbor, Debbie, (the neighborhood megaphone) was outside at her mailbox and walked over to say "hello." She looked just like a Barbie doll- skinny with her makeup and hair perfect, and I looked like Barbie's overweight, frumpy cousin: "Slobbie."

Debbie smiled at me through her dazzling white teeth. How did she get those SO white? Mine were like a color you'd find in a Crayola box. Like Macaroni and Cheese or Goldenrod. I was so distracted thinking about teeth that I didn't hear a word she said until Callie's name caught my attention.

"So you've heard about Callie, haven't you?"

"Huh? No. What?" I asked.

"They just filed for bankruptcy. They're probably going to lose their house. Isn't that just awful?"

I nodded my head, not knowing what to say because it really was awful.

"I guess now we know why she was selling all her things at that garage sale last month." Debbie seemed all too happy to share her "information." But all I could think of was how horrible Callie must feel and how hard things must be for her family right now.

Then with a sly smile she said, "I guess you just never really know what's going on inside somebody's house, do you?"

I just looked back at her and said where she could barely hear it, "Yeah. I guess not." The comment was more to myself than anyone else. I walked back toward the house. Debbie said, "Have a good day!!" in that sweet kindergarten teacher voice that made you think she was about to bend down and try to tie your shoes for you. I managed a smile and replied, "Yeah, you too."

As I entered my house, surveying boxes long forgotten, surrounded by the clutter of things that I had been saving for the day "that I might need it," an all too familiar shadow began to loom over my head. I knew where the feeling came from. I felt it every time I was in my house. It came from deep inside of me. I used to call it guilt, but it had grown into much more. It was sadness. It was hopelessness. Maybe this is what depression feels like.

I couldn't remember the last time I had not felt this way in this house. Then it hit me. I didn't feel this sadness when I saw my face in my shining sink! I remembered that feeling of hope. It was only a glimmer of hope, but that's more than what I'd had. That glimmer of the sink smiling at me made me smile back, and I knew I could shine that sink and keep it looking good. If there's hope in a shiny sink, then maybe there's hope for the rest of this house. Hope: that's a friend I hadn't previously had.

I walked into my living room and was looking at the pile of stuff that I had moved around earlier when something caught my eye. It was one of Ethan's favorite books perched on the very top of the pile. The picture on the front was what had caught my attention. I read it to him countless times when he was little, but he had outgrown it years ago. Some may call it a coincidence, but with everything that was going on in my life and then finding this book, I knew it was something more. "A God Breeze" as FlyLady called *it. The book was <u>The Little Engine That Could</u>. I thought about this simple title and realized, that's me! I was the little engine that could. I found a sticky note and along with my new friend, "Hope", I wrote out my new mantra: "I think I can! I think I can!"*

It was really good, but I knew Brittany and Dan would make fun of me for it. I had to come up with something that only I would know what it meant. Thinking back to the picture on the front that had drawn my attention in the first place, I decided instead of "I think I can! I think I can" to draw an engine on the sticky notes. With the way I draw, nobody would know what it was anyway. I drew out three small trains on sticky notes (that was all the sticky notes I had left). I put one in my car, one on the refrigerator, and one on the bathroom mirror.

From the de-clutter section in "<u>Sink Reflections</u>", I learned that three boxes would work just fine for getting rid of this mess in my house. One for a give-away box, one for a throw-away box, and one for a put-away box. I grabbed the first three boxes I saw and got started.

I decided to start in the kitchen so my counters would match my beautiful sink. I opened a drawer in my kitchen and found not two, not three, but FOUR ice cream scoops. Really?? Is there some occasion coming up where I'm going to have an ice cream eating contest and four scoops are required? This was an "ah-ha" moment for me. An epiphany from some ice cream scoops. Who would have thought such a thing was possible?

Of course, the reason I bought four in the first place was because I kept losing the one I had, buying a new one, and then finding the original one about a month later. I remember finding one buried in the backyard once. I think Ethan was using it to make cannonballs for his fort. There seems to be a pattern with things here: Five pairs of scissors, tape everywhere, (and yet I never could find it when I needed it) and I can't even count the number of flashlights and mismatched batteries. I'm pretty sure if there was a rainstorm and we lost power, I'd have enough to supply the entire neighborhood for a week! I was especially bad at buying multiple tools and gardening equipment for the house.

It hit me that this "having a place for things and keeping them there" would save us lots of money. As I thought of all these things, I kept hearing my guilt saying, "BUT you might need it someday." I saw it now for what it was: An excuse to keep us covered in clutter.

FlyLady said we could bless others with our abundance and have faith that if the day came when we needed it, God would provide. So, I took a leap of faith to provide for others. Well, I guess not quite a leap but it was a real baby step in the right direction. There are people in desperate need of these things that are overwhelming my family, my home, and me.

I remember hearing FlyLady say how one of her favorite places to take her abundance of stuff was to a charity that meets the needs of battered women and children. She told about how they often have to flee their homes in the middle of the night in their pajamas without even a change of clothes or shoes, nothing for the kids to wear, much less toys for them. These are the people I could be helping. These are the people that my abundance could be blessing.

Another of FlyLady's favorite places to donate was Habitat for Humanity. I took all my extra sets of tools and tool boxes (I had FIVE hammers!) to my local Habitat ReStore, as they call it. I also donated some building materials (nails and a window) that were left over from a remodeling project we did four years ago. They appreciated getting all these supplies and it made me feel great knowing it was going to a cause that would provide decent places to live for so many deserving people.

FlyLady said to declutter by removing 27 items at a time. She called it a 27 Fling Boogie. What a cute name! I set my timer for 15 minutes and got started with the counter to the right of the sink. There were lots of things that needed a home and I got bogged down trying to find a place to put things. Everywhere I looked it was already full! That's when it dawned on me: that's what the boxes were for. I filled up two throw-away boxes lined with garbage bags. (Yes, I finally went to the store to get them.) When one got full, I made myself stop and take it to the garbage can.

I was just getting into the swing of things when the timer started ringing loudly. It was time to stop. I have to confess, though, that the alarm going off every 15 minutes was really getting on my nerves! And I don't just mean the sound of the alarm. I mean having to stop after 15 minutes! There was so much more to do and just about the time I got some momentum that alarm would start to buzz!

Just as my timer began to buzz for the third time, I remembered I'd read somewhere that FlyLady had a special crisis cleaning method and I was definitely in a crisis. I set my timer again for 15 minutes to give myself time to learn about crisis cleaning. I Googled it and to my surprise, I found a great FlyLady video on YouTube where she crisis cleans her guest bedroom. She set the timer for 15 minutes and stayed focused on one area, then set the timer for another 15 minutes and decluttered a different area. She did this a third time, then rested for 15 minutes. She said the reason she did this was to keep from getting overwhelmed.

I began working on my kitchen the same way FlyLady did in the video. After three 15-minute decluttering sessions, it was time for a 15-minute break. Wait, I don't have time for a break, do I? But FlyLady said I should. I fixed a cup of tea, turned on some calm music and surveyed my work of the previous hour.

I could see some real progress! I had actually accomplished something. It was so wonderful to sip my tea and see my counter top not cluttered with papers, dishes and the kids' things. I knew I had to keep it that way and keep us all from piling it right back up. FlyLady had a great suggestion to put something pretty in the place that collects clutter. There was an old silver vase that was in the cabinet. It was a wedding gift from Dan's grandmother we had never used. I took it out and put it on the counter top. It looked like it belonged there. It was so pretty and it made me smile.

It took me several days to completely clean my kitchen, but using the 27 Fling Boogie really made it so much easier, and it was actually fun! I am absolutely amazed at the progress I've made in these last few weeks. As I surveyed my beautiful, clean kitchen, somehow I KNOW I can. I looked at that little engine on my refrigerator and smiled at it. I was actually proud of what I had done. No, that's not quite right... I was proud of ME. A phrase suddenly popped into my mind.... Go Me!

Chapter 5
Starting Small, Slow, and Steady

Dear Diary,

I know it's been a long time. Could there possibly be anything more we could fit into a summer? Baseball games, swimming parties, Vacation Bible School, youth camps, family vacation, going to visit relatives... It seemed like there was something to do every day of every week!

I had let the summer get in the way of my new routine. I really didn't mean for it to happen, but gradually other things just took over. I was cleaning my sink and making a dent in the clutter, but once summer hit, morning routines didn't seem very urgent. Little by little, my routines slipped away from me.

Then we went on vacation for a week and my routines were just gone. I never picked them back up and I had been doing SO well! The next thing I knew, one week had turned into a month. Then two months. Then suddenly the entire summer was gone and it was time for school to begin again. As silently as dust bunnies form under the bed, clutter stacked up again.

It wasn't like I did nothing. That's NOT the case at all. I started a scrapbooking hobby, volunteered as a team mom for Ethan's baseball team and the kids and I even worked on the yard and planted some flowers in front of the house. We had to clear out a few weeds, but we enjoyed just spending some time together.

As the summer was now drawing to a close, I looked at my kitchen and remembered back to the days that I had clean counters and a sparkling sink. I remembered the sense of accomplishment that I had felt as I looked at it back then. I had been so proud of myself and all of my hard work. Now it was right back where it started, and I didn't feel the least bit proud of myself. Well, maybe it wasn't quite as messy as before, but I had definitely fallen off the FlyLady bandwagon. I needed to get back into a routine and now I really wanted it for myself... not just to please everyone else. I wanted that feeling of peace and accomplishment that I had when I first shined my sink. I wanted to live in a clean house and feel like I truly had a home.

You know, it's the strangest thing that when things seem impossible, a solution appears that starts something you never expected. All three kids are in different schools this year, with three different calendars. This year there was no way I could keep up with everything unless I had it written down in one place.

I had to go get school supplies for Ethan and Karly today so I thought while I was there I would look for a big family calendar. I took Ethan shopping with me. He loves buying office supplies just like me and he is always a pleasure to be around.

While we were shopping, I ran into my friend, Susan. Ethan and her son played on the same baseball team this summer; so Susan and I had seen each other often. Corey came running up to Ethan and high-fived him. In a blur, they ran off to the video game section together while we both yelled after them, "Stop running in the store!"

Susan looked at me with a big smile that was as genuine as everything else about her and said, "Boys will be boys! Gina, it's so good to see you!"

Gina! So that's the name of the lady writing the diary!

Susan was always so sweet. Peace and joy seemed to surround her like a warm bubble bath. As a matter of fact, she always seemed to find joy in everything she did. She always looked great, too. Even when she had on a pair of shorts, and her hair was pulled back in a ponytail, she looked put together and her skin was radiant! I could never tell if she was wearing makeup or not, but she always looked beautiful. And here I was looking like a dirty dishrag. My appearance was definitely something I needed to add to my routines.

Susan asked, "I see you're taking advantage of the back to school sale, too." I smiled and nodded yes. "They always have the best prices here. Oh my goodness! I love your shoes!"

"Thank you!" I replied. "Karly picked them out for me. She thought they were pretty."

"She was right, they are very pretty. What all are you going to have to buy this year?" Susan asked as she pulled out her shopping list. I, of course, didn't have a list at all, so I replied, "Just the usual stuff."

We walked through the store talking about the kids while putting things in our shopping carts. She was so easy to talk to and always had an encouraging word to say. As I watched Susan shop, it helped me remember a few things I needed. Everything Susan threw into her cart, I also threw into mine. I figured her list was good enough for my kids, too, and since they were about the same ages, it had to be close!

We came to the aisle with the wall calendars. I picked up a few of them, but they were too small, or the actual dates were too small for me to write in them. I needed something larger to write all the kids' information, not to mention mine. Susan must've been reading my face and asked, "What's wrong?"

43

"I need to get a wall calendar to help me organize my home, but I need a really big space for all I have to keep up with."

Susan smiled and replied, "I know exactly how you feel. I had the same problem for years until I found a calendar online. Have you ever heard of the FlyLady?"

What were the chances of that? I know my face had to tell her I was surprised to hear her mention FlyLady as I responded, "Yes, I have! I've read her book <u>Sink Reflections</u>."

"Oh! Isn't she great? I get her emails every day! She has a calendar you can purchase right off her website with spaces big enough to keep up with a family. I actually have one, if you want to see what it looks like. It has the cutest stickers for keeping up with things like doctor appointments and vacations."

I stood there nodding my head wishing I had kept up with my routines. "Thank you so much, Susan. I think I will give her calendar a try. It's got to be better than the scraps of paper I've been using. But, what's this about emails from FlyLady?"

"Oh! Well, she sends out emails every day on everything from decluttering to attitude adjustments. They help me to understand how the routines work in real life. A lot of them are written by members who are just like me, and it's all free. I'm not sure how they do it but there is never a charge for it."

Note to self: Get on the FlyLady email list!

I asked Susan, "Do you follow the FlyLady's routines, too?"

"Oh, girl! I couldn't live without them! They've changed my whole life!"

"Did you have trouble fitting them all into your schedule?" I asked.

"The funny part is," Susan laughed as she said, "the routines give you time to do all the fun things you never had time to do before, as long as you don't try to do everything at the same time. Start out de-cluttering and take one thing at a time until they gradually become a part of your daily routines."

"How can more work give me more free time?" I asked with a puzzled look.

"It's not more work. It's actually less but I can see how it can be confusing for you. We have just GOT to get together and talk. You're not going to believe how easy this is!" Susan replied.

I smiled and thanked her. We finished our shopping and as we parted ways in the parking lot, Susan called to me, "Remember, Gina: Baby Steps! And don't forget to call me so we can get together this week!" I knew she meant it. I thanked her, then Ethan and I got in the car and headed home.

After unloading the bags from the car, I got on the computer and found the FlyLady calendar. It was a lot more affordable than I thought it would be. I couldn't wait for it to get here so I could start adding my routines to the calendar. In the meantime, I decided to look on the website for information about the Baby Steps. I found the 31 Baby Steps right away. Great! I thought they looked like a lot of work until I realized I was only supposed to add one Baby Step per day.

This time I was not going to burn out. As I looked at ALL these steps, I remembered FlyLady's words: "Slow and steady wins the race." I knew I could shine my sink so that was my goal for the day... and I did it.

45

The next morning I got "dressed to my lace up shoes" and brushed my frizzy hair until it looked manageable. Normally my hair was a barometer for bad weather. You could look at it and tell how close a storm was, but I was proud to say on that day, it looked quite good. Karly even commented on my "pretty hair."

The calendar arrived much faster than I anticipated. I was excited! Susan was right: There was plenty of space for me to write. I was starting to settle back into my 15 minute decluttering sessions and I was even beginning to see some changes.

My nature is to jump in and try to do everything at once, but I remembered this usually leads me to major burnout and eventually to a bag of peanut M&M's. So I decided to simply take my calendar and I wrote one of the 31 Baby Steps on each day. I shined my sink with a sense of hope. I smiled when I saw the sticky note with the picture of the Little Engine That Could, and headed to bed at a decent time.

At first I felt a little guilty about only doing a few things a day, but Susan reinforced the value in these "Baby Steps." Just one step a day, slow and steady... It was easier for me to add a little at a time.

UPDATE: I did really well the first eight days. But then Ethan got sick and I was taking care of him and I had a few other things come up. I just couldn't do it. Now I'm behind and feel like I can't just pick back up in the middle of the month. WHY didn't I follow through?

I called Susan and talked to her about it. She told me something that really helped me. She said that when she felt behind, she read at the bottom of a FlyLady email, "You are not behind. Just jump in where we are."

I took this to heart and started again. It was day 17, but it didn't matter. I started there and pretty much made it straight through to day 31. Susan called me at the end of the month and told me how proud of me she was for picking myself back up, and for starting where I was and following through. I have to admit, it felt pretty good.

I thought to myself, "Life is getting better!!"

Chapter 6
The Table

Dear Diary,

I had woken up 30 minutes earlier than normal because I had set my alarm. I was thinking about my calendar and what my Baby Step was going to be today. I got up, got in the shower, got dressed and fixed my hair. I even smiled at myself in the mirror. I can't even remember how long it had been since I had smiled at an image of myself. For a fluffy mom of three, I didn't look half bad.

I walked out of the bathroom to go downstairs when I heard the yelling. It sounded serious, so I ran downstairs to find Ethan and Karly arguing over who would get to eat the last Pop Tart. I had forgotten to pick up another box yesterday.

Dan glared at me and sarcastically quipped, "Let me guess: You didn't have time to get the grocery store? I suppose that's what happened to the milk that isn't in our refrigerator either. Since I only have to work 12 hours today so you can stay home and 'Clean the house' should I make time myself to go to the grocery store, Oh domestic goddess of mine?"

"No" I sheepishly replied. I felt like digging a hole deeper than the one my life already resided in and hiding, but I quietly replied, "I'll take care of it."

Dan stood, picked up his briefcase and as he turned to walk out the door said, "That's what you said yesterday, too. That's what you always say," as he slammed the door for an exclamation point. I stood there in the deafening silence staring at the door, tears welling up in my eyes. I was not going to let this defeat me.

I looked down to see Ethan and Karly staring at me to decide who the proud owner of the last Pop Tart in our house would be. For a moment I thought I would be like Solomon and split it in half and the rightful owner wouldn't let me sacrifice the last precious Pop Tart, but then it hit me: School didn't start for another few days so we would celebrate the new beginning with a trip to the Breakfast Barn! This was immediately met with a cheer. Why not? I was dressed and ready to go. I yelled up the stairs to see if, by some miracle, Brittany would want to join us, but the silence told me she was still asleep.

As we drove to the Breakfast Barn, Dan's words were still stinging me. "That's what you always say." He didn't trust me anymore. My words meant nothing to him. We were growing distant and I knew it was because of all this. We sat down at "The Barn" and ate a monstrous spread of eggs, pancakes, bacon, sausage, biscuits, fruit, and donuts. I was still mulling over everything Dan had said. His words stressed me out worse than anything. I started feeling a migraine coming on. I had to stop eating. I knew if my migraine went to full blown status, I was going to be sick at my stomach, too.

Brittany glared at me when we returned to the house. I could tell she was in one of her moods. "Are you aware we're out of milk AND eggs?"

"I'm going to the grocery store later today", I said.

Karly jumped in "We just went to the Breakfast Barn and ate the whole buffet!"

"Great, Mom! Yeah, I guess you couldn't have picked up anything for ME while you were taking everybody else out to eat, could you?" she replied sarcastically. She was definitely her father's daughter and becoming more like him every day.

"I called upstairs to see if you wanted to go and you didn't answer," I calmly replied.

With her famous roll of the eyes, she replied, "AS IF I would want that junk."

Ethan offered, "There's one Pop Tart left!"

"I don't want a Pop Tart, Nate. I'd like to have some food in the refrigerator for a change but I guess that's too much to ask. ."

A spark of anger rose up in me. "Look, Brittany! I'm going to the grocery store today. One day without eggs is NOT going to kill you."

"Whatever, Mom." She stomped out of the room.

I was sick of fighting with Brittany. But I was even sicker of how she talked to me so disrespectfully. I followed her into the living room and said, "You will NOT talk to me that way anymore! I'm tired of it. I'm your mother and you WILL treat me with respect."

"Respect? REALLY?? Respect?" Brittany shouted. "How can I respect someone who doesn't respect herself or her family? Look at this mess, and look at YOU!"

"That's enough!" I screamed. It was so loud the dog started barking outside. I calmed my voice and continued, "I realize I'm not perfect, but neither are you. I'm working on making some changes. You just have to be patient."

With a sarcastic smirk, Brittany shot back, "Changes are coming? How many times have we heard that, Mom? How many times? How is this any different from when you said you were going to

51

change before? From when you started cleaning up the kitchen and then quit two weeks later? From when you started the weight loss program and signed up for eight weeks and quit after only a week? How about when you got into that multi-level marketing business that sold candy that made you lose weight? Or like all this scrapbooking stuff that's on the floor now that you're never going to finish?"

She had just thrown my life back in my face and the truth was devastating. Even Brittany with her hard-nosed approach sensed my grief because her next phrase was spoken with a more comforting tone, although it was the most devastating phrase of all:

"Look, Mom, some people are just not made to be organized and you're one of them. The sooner you can face that, the better off all of us will be and the sooner we'll find a real solution to this mess we live in." She walked back into the kitchen. I walked up the stairs to my bedroom, shut the door, and cried.

Again, my daughter had now taken on the role of the parent. She was right. I knew it. She knew it. I just wasn't made to be organized. But I was organized when I was in high school and college. I helped organize an office when I first started working. What had happened to me? Kids came along and I seemed to lose that ability.

The rest of the day was a blur. At some point I called Susan to take her up on her offer to talk. She invited me over for the afternoon. I could certainly use some time away from here and it had been a long time since I had taken time for myself. Once the kids came along, I had gradually isolated myself in the house away from the rest of the world. I had eliminated all my friends, not on purpose, but by sheer neglect.

Her house was sitting a little way off the road and the drive was lined with Weeping Willow trees. It had a finely manicured yard with several small gardens bursting with flowers of red, bright orange, and cheery yellow.

I was filled with mixed emotions as I walked to her front door. How could anyone with a life like this possibly understand what my life was like and what I was dealing with?

Before I could ring the doorbell, or change my mind and run, Susan opened the door, gave me a smile and a hug, and said, "Come on in, Gina."

Susan's house was homey. The two story foyer was open, yet intimate in a way that seemed to wrap its arms around you in a welcoming hug, just like Susan. Everything was in its place and everything had a place. I'm not saying it was perfect; it was lived in. Her home was a place of peace and joy. There was a book on the table that looked like it was just supposed to be there. As I glanced at her living room, I felt like I was in the story of Goldilocks. There was an obviously comfortable leather chair with a newspaper near it for her husband, along with an ottoman for his feet. There was a large, overstuffed fluffy chair covered in chintz of pink roses. The throw over the chair was a pink, chenille blanket and I also noticed a book in the chair, _Body Clutter_, by the FlyLady and Leanne Ely. I made a mental note to pick that up later.

Even looking at Susan made me feel bad. She wasn't trying to make me feel bad, mind you. She was nothing but kind and sweet. She seemed so calm and at peace with her entire world. It wasn't even 10:00 AM and she had on a cute outfit with her hair and makeup fixed. My head was hurting worse. We sat down in Susan's living room. I could barely look at her. I felt so inferior and full of shame. Why couldn't I get my life together like she obviously had?

I noticed her coffee table was unique. It was a wooden shadow box table with a glass display case in a Feng Shui design. Looking through the glass, there was sand all along the bottom of the display case and there were several curious items placed inside.

Susan sat down next to me, put her hand on my arm and then smiled reassuringly as she said, "Ok, Gina. What's going on?"

I finally blurted out, "My life is a wreck!" I burst into tears. I couldn't believe it, but I did. Susan sat there looking at me empathetically waiting for me to go on, so I continued, "It's Dan. It's my kids. It's my house. It's my EVERYTHING. I can't get anything done. I take two steps forward and three steps back. I hate my life and myself!"

"But, Gina, you're a wonderful person and a great mother. Your kids love you. I've watched them around you."

"Well," I muttered, "Maybe Karly and Ethan do, but Brittany is so bitter and angry."

"How old is she now?" asked Susan.

"15 going on 40."

Susan smiled, "Sounds like a typical teenager to me."

I explained, "She acts like she's the adult. She's correcting me and the thing is she's right."

"About what?"

"I'm really embarrassed to say."

Susan reassured me, "It's ok. I want to help."

"It's my house. It's a wreck. It looks like a bomb went off in it. I've tried to get it organized but no matter what I do, nothing seems to work. You mentioned the FlyLady stuff to me. I did order that calendar by the way, but I just don't think I'm made to be organized or have a clean house! Brittany told me that she thinks I'm one of those people who just aren't capable of being organized."

Susan said, "That's not true, Gina. You CAN do this. If I did it, anybody can."

"You?? But you're as close to perfect as you can get."

"Perfect?" Susan laughed out loud. "There's no such thing as perfect. There's only progress."

I continued, "No! Really! Just look at you. Your hair, your makeup, your house. Everything is in its place! I feel like such a failure!"

"Well, it wasn't always that way. In fact, if you had seen my house four years ago, you definitely wouldn't feel that way," Susan said.

I had to know so I asked, "What do you mean?"

Susan began telling me, "Well, four years ago my house and my life were a wreck. In fact, it was a disaster. There was one time the police came to my house to ask for money for their annual fundraiser and the officer actually asked me if my house had been broken into and ransacked."

"What???? You're kidding me!"

"No, no," Susan said. "He even asked me if anything had been stolen!"

"Oh, yeah..." she continued, "I had so much junk in my yard, people would sometimes stop and ask me if I was having a yard sale. My husband told me that he couldn't stand to be here. He worked longer hours at the office to keep from coming home to the chaos and we fought constantly. I'm telling you, Gina. I've been right where you are and there IS a solution."

"How? How did you do it?" I asked her.

"Well," Susan said, pointing to an odd looking table, it was some kind of display case with a glass top that allowed you to see inside. "My FlyLady journey is laid out right in front of you."

Pointing to a cluster of objects she continued, "This jumbled mess represents the clutter that was my life and my home. I was living in complete and utter chaos and was about to end up in a divorce. I was about to lose custody of my children and my self esteem was as low as it could get."

Then Susan pointed to the rocks leading away from the mess and said they were stepping-stones. The rocks were all different shapes and they formed a path leading away from the clutter. I asked Susan, "How could these possibly work as stepping stones?"

Susan smiled and said, "You're very observant. The stepping-stones represent my routines and as I used them, the jagged edges smoothed away and became a part of my life. Many times I fell off the wagon from doing my routines (my stepping-stones), but I got back up and kept going."

I jumped ahead of Susan now, wanting to know more about the items. The next one was a sundial with a lot of stones surrounding it and the number 31 drawn in the sand in the center. The stones were all different colors and I had to know, "What is the sundial for?"

"The sundial represents FlyLady's 31 Baby Steps that started my journey out of chaos. See the silver stone? That's my sink being shined. The red one represents the hot spots I cleaned up and I still do!" she added with a laugh.

I spotted a small hourglass and pointed to it, "Is this one for decluttering 15 minutes a day?" Susan nodded, "Yes."

Next to the sundial was some more stones leading to 12 small, silver bars in the shape of a triangle with four bars on each side. "And these? What are these?" I asked.

"Those are the 12 monthly habits. Where would you say the beginning of the triangle is?" Susan asked.

I looked at the bars. How could you tell where the beginning of a triangle was? Who was to say it was the top or the sides? I just admitted, "I don't know."

"Exactly!" replied Susan. "These 12 habits really don't have a beginning. You just jump in wherever you are. That's going to be important for you to remember. Also, notice they are silver bars. Silver is a precious metal and even though it looks rigid, when the heat is applied, it becomes flexible just like your routines. You make them fit your life. You make them your own, especially when the heat is turned up on your life. That's when they are most important."

Last of all were some flat stones that were a bit concave, very smooth and worn from lots of use.

"Ok," I asked, pointing at them "What are these?"

"These are the steps that I took to establish routines to fit my house, my family and my life."

I had to really look twice to catch what was on the far right. At first it looked just like sand. But as I looked closer I saw some shiny, colorful, crushed stones that might have even been jewels. There were other items arranged in a way that resembled shells that had been washed ashore on the beach.

Susan saw me looking and explained, "This represents the peaceful and serene life that I have achieved. If you're wondering what all those things are that are crushed in the sand, they are essentially the same things you see on the far left. Most of the stones we've collected over the years. Amethyst that the kids found on a vacation, garnet from my grandmother's broken ring, and onyx and rose quartz from my mother's jewelry box. There's even some ground up gold from an old necklace.

By eliminating clutter and keeping what was beautiful and functional, my life began to flow and actually became peaceful. It made me who I am today. This is the journey. It isn't even really about a clean house. It's about a life that is uncluttered and happy."

As I stared at all that Susan had accomplished, I asked, "Could I really get to this point?"

Susan immediately answered, "Of course you can! But remember, my house did not get clean over night. It took months of decluttering and establishing basic routines, and I did it all with Baby Steps."

"I read about those on FlyLady's website, but they seem so simple! How could they possibly help me dig my way out of all MY clutter?"

Susan smiled and replied, "That's what is so unique about the system. It is simple! It's the simplicity and you being consistent with those Baby Steps that gets the chaos out of your life. It's all up to you to do the work."

"Well, Susan, what's the first step? Where do I even begin?"

"Oh that's easy! We start with shining our sink. Have you done that yet?"

"Yes, but that doesn't really compare to what you've done. Whatever I do never seems to help. It's like a drop of water in the ocean, it doesn't make a bit of difference. And I..."

"Whoa, whoa, whoa!" Susan interrupted, "That's GREAT. You've shined your sink. That's step one! You've taken a step in the right direction. I can remember there was a time when the only clean thing in my house WAS my sink. We all have to start somewhere. It starts with those small Baby Steps. Remember to give yourself some credit. Don't keep beating yourself up!"

"You know, now that you mention it, I did get out my FlyLady calendar and wrote my 31 Baby Steps on it. I even managed to make it through most of them, and they weren't all that hard. The hardest part was remembering to do them, but my calendar kept me on track. Every time I realized that I had missed a day, I wanted to trash the whole thing. I felt so far behind already. I should have started this in January."

"That's the beauty of the system. It's like my triangle with no beginning and no end: you can start anytime and anywhere.

There's not a set time to begin. FlyLady always says in her emails, 'You're not behind, just jump in where we are." Susan leaned in and took my hand and said, "Gina, you're not behind. Just jump in where YOU are. And Gina," she added, "If I can do it, you can do it, too. If you don't quit."

I smiled a smile of hope. "Thank you, Susan."

"Don't thank me yet. I haven't done anything! Let's get started with what you're going to do now.

"Now that you've finished the Baby Steps, let's start working on FlyLady's Monthly Habit."

"What is this month's habit?" I asked.

Susan replied, "It's the before bedtime routine. Have you heard of that?"

I replied, "Yes. I've actually written one out. I think it's still on a sticky note on my mirror."

"Ok. All I want you to do next is write out your monthly habit at the top of each month of your FlyLady calendar, continue to keep your sink shiny, and work on your before bedtime routine."

"That's it?" I asked with a bewildered look.

"Yep. That's it. Baby Steps, Gina. Small steps lead to great journeys. You'll get there. Just take your time and don't give up. As FlyLady says, 'Slow and steady wins the race.' Even if you miss a day or two, pick up and keep going." Susan's tone gave me encouragement and hope.

I went home and read over all of FlyLady's monthly habits for the year. They were:

January:	Shining Your Sink
February:	Declutter for 15 minutes
March:	Getting dressed to shoes
April:	Making your bed
May:	Moving in May
June:	Drinking Your Water
July:	Swish and Swipe
August:	Laundry
September:	Before bed routine
October:	Paper clutter
November:	Menu planning
December:	Pampering

I didn't know what all these meant. I wasn't sure how I could only emphasize laundry for one month out of the year, but oh, well. I'm sure the FlyLady knew what she was doing, and I followed her directions. I even started singing a little song:

Baby Steps, baby steps, aaaaaall day.
Baby steps, baby steps, show the way.
Baby steps, baby steps, here we go
Baby steps, baby steps, I'm on a roll!

I wrote out the habit for each month on my beautiful calendar and I actually felt pretty good about doing what Susan had said to do.

I remember her telling me that she had gone to see the FlyLady in person at a conference! She said she took some questions from the audience and one of the Fly babies (Yes, of course I had to interrupt her and find out what in the world a Flybaby was! Come to find out, it's a name the members of her website had picked for themselves. Too cute!) asked what's the main reason people don't *succeed in their routines? She had told them that the main downfall was people DON'T DECLUTTER. She told them that it took her decluttering 27 things, 3 times a day for nine months. I thought to myself, "Seriously? Nine months?" This encouraged me because I realized this race was not a sprint; it was a marathon! And other people like FlyLady, Susan, and millions of FlyBabies had run this race successfully before me. If they could do it, there was no reason I couldn't do it, too.*

It was time for me to start decluttering. I thought it would be difficult, but when I realized that everything in my house (including trash!) counted as an item, it wasn't difficult... especially with my house! Decluttering meant that I could give away, throw away, or put away 27 items. You know, that might just be fun!

My basic routine for the month was to declutter three times a day. Which took about five minutes or less. Yes, I was amazed too! I also was going to do my before bedtime routine and to keep my sink clean and shiny.

I can do this!

Chapter 7
Paper Clutter

Dear Diary,

This month, we are going to focus on our paper clutter.

Ugh. That's a bad one for me. In science they say the body is 90% water. I'm pretty sure my house is 90% paper clutter. I really wasn't sure what was clutter and what wasn't clutter so, I kept EVERYTHING. I called Susan to ask her opinion.

"A few years ago, I needed help with that, too. How about if I come over and help you define what is and isn't paper clutter?"

My heart rate must have jumped to 200 beats per minute. I could feel my stomach drop to my toes just at the very thought of her or anyone else seeing the inside of my house. "That's very sweet of you, but I think I can do it if you just tell me how."

"Oh, honey, I know how it is to have C.H.A.O.S. like FlyLady talks about. You know, CHAOS stands for 'Can't Have Anybody Over Syndrome?' I was the poster child for CHAOS! As a matter of fact, let me email you a picture of my living room that Dennis took several years ago."

There was no way I was letting her come over. I didn't care what she said. It wasn't going to happen. Susan was still talking, "I just emailed it to you. Did you get it?"

I walked over to the computer and opened my email. I couldn't believe my eyes. It looked like a bomb had gone off in their living room. There were papers everywhere. There was no arrangement to anything in the room. The table, if you could really call it that, was sideways and covered with opened cereal boxes, magazines, popcorn bags, and it looked as if someone had spilled some cereal on the table and it had spilled onto the floor. Or... maybe it was popcorn. I couldn't really tell. Surrounding the room and in the middle of the floor were stacks of boxes that made a small path through the middle of the room. It looked like a filthy warehouse instead of a living room. There were mounds of clothes on the floor and furniture. I could see a small space on the couch that was severely dented and looked like the space where someone usually sat. I suppose it was because it was the only place anybody in the room actually could sit. As I looked at this picture of pure CHAOS, a single "Ohhhhh" escaped from my thoughts and into the phone.

I evidently said it louder than I thought I had because Susan replied, "Now you see what the routines have done for me. I was paralyzed and had no clue where to begin. But just like you, I started with Baby Steps, decluttering, and the monthly focus. Like I said, I did it and so can you. Paper clutter was one of my hardest habits too. How bad is yours?"

"Bad," I replied. Then without thinking I said, "I mean not as bad as this picture but... OH! I'm sorry! I didn't mean that, I just meant..." Oh my. Talk about sticking my foot in my mouth!

Susan was laughing. "It's ok. It was bad. I just wanted you to see it so you would know that the routines and decluttering really do work."

"Thank you for sending me that picture," I replied. "I know it must have been hard to share that with me. I can't imagine being able to show anyone my house right now."

"You're welcome. Now, go on FlyLady.net and search for paper clutter. You'll find a list of 20 or so things that constitute clutter and how to deal with them. This month all FlyLady wants you to

do is the 31 Baby Steps, continue your before bedtime routine, and declutter your paper. That's it."

"I can do that," I said. I thanked Susan again before we hung up, then I went on the FlyLady website and found her list of paper clutter. They were:

1. Piles of newspapers.
2. Baskets of unread magazines.
3. Junk mail.
4. Boxes of your old school papers and your kids' artwork.
5. Recipes.
6. Paperback books.
7. Piles of unopened mail.
8. Tax papers.
9. Medical records.
10. Paid bills receipts. (You don't need it. It's on your bank statements ONLINE.)
11. Old phone books.
12. CATALOGS .
13. Bank statements.
14. File cabinets full of who knows what!
15. Family pictures.
16. Birth certificates.
17. Purses full of STUFF.
18. Maps.
19. Travel brochures.
20. Organizational books.
21. Computer printouts from FlyLady email and other websites.
22. 3x5 cards.
23. Other office supplies we are addicted to. File folders, dividers.

I dove right in. I thought my purse would be an easier place to start. My purse resembled George Costanza's wallet on "Seinfeld." I had so much stuff jammed in there that it was practically spring loaded. I began to dig through and pull out all sorts of things that made me wonder how they had gotten in there. No wonder I never could find anything in my purse! Two brushes, a broken powder compact (which I never used), receipts from two years ago... scratch that... THREE years ago. Kleenex, some folded, some crumpled. Ewwww!

After getting frustrated with digging in the purse, I dumped the contents onto the floor. How did I accumulate this much junk? I looked in the bottom of the purse to see if everything was out. There were still two suckers stuck to the bottom of my purse. I suppose that explained the stuffy, cherry aroma that I had smelled whenever I wrote a check. I still wasn't sure what I was going to do with a few items in the purse. More on that later...

Newspapers and magazines were easy to find. Why in the world did I keep all these newspapers? I guess it was because I felt bad for throwing away something I had paid for and hadn't read. But then again, if I hadn't read it, did I really need to get it in the first place? I could probably get my news online for free and SAVE some money.

Magazines weren't in baskets in my house. They were in BOXES. I had National Geographics and TV Guides from 15 years ago. I didn't see any of them selling on eBay for big bucks, and easily tossed them in the trash. Definitely throw-aways! I decided I needed a throw-away recycle box for a lot of this paper clutter!

I didn't have trouble throwing out junk mail. I just had to find all of it. The first several days it was easy to find. It was lying on my kitchen counters, living room and bedroom floors and tables, as well as the sink in my downstairs bathroom. How in the world it made it in there was beyond me. As the month kept going I had to search a little harder for it. I was also amazed at some of the unopened mail I had kept. How important could these letters be if I *had them for six months and hadn't opened them? Time to shred and recycle.*

I found four years' worth of old phone books and tossed them into the box, as well as catalogs from years and years ago. FlyLady said if I wasn't going to place an order in the next day or two, then I needed to get rid of them, since they were usually available online anyway. There were some old travel brochures of places I wanted to go. Most of them were way out of date anyway. Stacks and stacks of computer printouts ranging from articles to things the kids had printed out and long since forgotten were tossed in the recycle box, too.

I also went through bookshelves and boxes to find paperback books from years past that I had not ever read. I read somewhere that old books on shelves are very difficult to dust and that dust can create health problems for your family. Rather than just throw these away, though, I put them in some boxes and marked them to go to a charity store that donated used books to veteran organizations. It felt really good to let those go for such a worthy cause.

I took a look inside my file cabinet, but decided I would have to talk to Dan before I could really do anything with it. Tax papers, bill receipts, bank statements, and medical bills were things I was going to have to come back to. I was too scared of what Dan would say to throw those types of things away. Family pictures and birth certificates certainly seemed precious. I would have to ask Susan what to do with those.

By the end of two weeks, I had gotten rid of quite a bit of stuff. The next thing was the boxes of school papers. I opened them up and took a 10-year trip down memory lane: The kids' artwork from kindergarten, and tests they took two years ago. It was great to look at, but did I really need to keep it? FlyLady said I could keep some of the artwork and put it in a scrapbook or I could give some of it

67

away to the grandparents. This turned out to be a big hit with Nana and Pop. Besides, if I kept everything they did, it wouldn't be as special.

It was hard but I came to grips with the fact that most of these papers really didn't need to be saved. Karly was watching me throw some papers away. I was a little teary eyed when I threw one of her drawings away. She said, "It's ok, Mommy, I'll draw you a new one. Besides, I'm a MUCH better drawer now." It made me laugh. I hugged her and said, "Yes, you are a wonderful drawer!"

As I looked at what I had done, as far as decluttering papers, it didn't seem like I had accomplished much. I had easily thrown away 12 bags of papers, but the difference was barely noticeable. Was I just trying to organize clutter? Frustrated, I called Susan. Ever the encourager she told me to hang in there and keep going, "Slow and steady wins the race!" I needed to hear that phrase over and over.

I was frustrated though as I told her, "I've been working. I have the book. I've read the book! I have the calendar! I've written everything on the calendar and my house still isn't clean!"

Calmly, Susan replied, "Gina, remember what FlyLady said. Your house did not get dirty overnight, and it is not going to get clean in a day. You need to quit looking at what you haven't accomplished and concentrate on what you have. You're doing the Baby Steps, you're doing your before bedtime routine, and decluttering the paper will happen. It just takes time! You ARE making progress. I do want you to remember something, though. The FlyLady books and calendars are not the magic pill that suddenly makes your life organized and your house clean."

"I know," I replied. "There are no magic pills."

"Actually, in this case there is a magic pill."

"What is it?" I asked, desperate to know.

"It's actually pretty simple. It's your routines. Just going through your routines and... NOT GIVING UP."

She was right. I knew she was right. I thanked her.

Then she said, "Over my sink, I have this quote: 'Let us not grow weary in doing good for at the proper time we will reap a harvest if we do not give up.' Gina, don't give up. You're going to make it!"

After we talked I had a new resolve. The last week of October was spent going back to the piles of clutter that I had tried to organize. When I reevaluated what I had kept, I saw the clutter for what it was and I filed it in FlyLady's favorite place to put paper clutter: the garbage can.

At the end of the month, I could see some real progress. I put the recipes in a box. I sorted through them to find only my favorites and threw away the rest. I put the medical records in their own file.

FlyLady suggested getting a fireproof safe to put birth certificates and other valuable objects in. I wasn't sure where to get one, so I made copies of them and then put the originals in our safety deposit box at the bank for the time being. I realized all this wasn't a perfect way to organize this stuff, but it certainly looked better in those boxes than it did on the floor and on my tables. I just kept telling myself "Slow and steady wins the race!"

Decluttering three times a day, throwing the paper away, my before bedtime routine, and the 31 Baby steps had really made a dent in my house. Maybe there was light at the end of this tunnel after all.

Chapter 8
The Bird

Dear Diary,

We had a minor crisis that started about a month ago when Ethan was playing in our front yard. He noticed a baby bird lying at the foot of one of our trees. He came running indoors in tears saying there was a hurt baby bird outside that needed our help. He is so incredibly tenderhearted.

I walked outside to see the bird and see what I could do to help. It was so tiny and helpless. It didn't even make a peep as it lay there. His breathing was shallow and it didn't have any feathers on its little body. I looked around for its mother, but didn't see a bird anywhere nearby. Ethan sat there staring at me through tears desperate for me to "fix" this.

Karly helped us find its nest. It looked like the storm last night had knocked it over. Poor little bird. It was lying there dying. I just couldn't let that happen. It would absolutely crush Ethan! I had been told all my life that handling birds would cause the mother to abandon them, but when I Googled it, (what did we ever do before Google?) it said that was just an old wives' tale.

I got out a ladder, then carefully picked up the baby bird, and set it back in the nest. I made sure the nest was upright this time. The bird was back in the nest. Ethan calmed down. All was well.

That is, until last week. Ethan came running in after dinner and told me, "The bird is back on the ground! The bird is back on the ground! Come quick!"

It was almost dark, so I carefully walked over to where Ethan was pointing. Nate was right. The poor bird was back on the ground, way over in the middle of our driveway! It had grown. Now it was a little fuzzball. I reached down to see if it was alive and when my hand got near him, its neck stretched upward and its mouth opened wide. It began doing that hungry little bird peep over and over again.

Ethan chimed in, "We gotta feed him, mom! He's hungry!"

But what? I didn't know what to feed a bird. I was looking at the nest. It wasn't really tipped over at all. I was thinking about how in the world this could have happened again, when I realized Ethan was at my feet. He had evidently been digging through the flowerbed and had managed to dig up an earthworm. Ew! Typical boy!

I wasn't going to let Ethan touch the bird, so I made him put the worm down and sent him inside to get the tweezers. He returned quickly and for the first time in my life, I fed a bird... worms.

It was completely dark and there was no way I could see the nest, much less climb up there. Besides, it was time for us to go to bed. I told Nate to get ready for bed. He walked slowly toward the house turning to look over his shoulder at the bird several times. The next thing I knew, Karly came running downstairs to announce, "Ethan's crying!"

I went upstairs to find out what the problem was. As I walked through his bedroom door, Ethan said through his tears, "The bird's gonna die tonight! I just know it! The neighbor's mean cat is gonna eat him!"

I tried to assure him it wouldn't happen. He innocently but directly said, "Do you promise, mom?" How could I promise such a thing?

So... as any good parent would do, I dragged myself back downstairs to find a box, (in my house it wasn't very difficult) put some twigs and leaves in it, and gently put the bird into it and moved him into the garage where it was safe and warm. Ethan wanted him in the house, but I drew the line and said "Wild birds don't belong inside, Nate."

The next morning I awoke to Ethan in my face saying, "The bird's still in the box. He's ok!"

I groggily got up and walked in the garage to find what he said was true. I told Ethan, "Ok, now we put him back in his nest and let his mother take care of him."

We got out the ladder, climbed back up, and carefully placed the bird back in the nest. He was peeping away the entire time. I was going through my morning routine. Ethan wanted to get back outside to make sure the bird was ok. The next thing I knew, Ethan was yelling, "Mom! He's on the ground again!"

I couldn't believe it! I walked outside to find out, sure enough, that bird was BACK on the ground! I told Nate he was supposed to be there and to just leave him be. I was hoping we could move past this, and we were; that is, until Ethan came running in screaming, "Mom! Mom! Matthew kicked the bird! Matthew kicked the bird!" Matthew was the neighborhood bratty kid.

I ran outside to find the bird in a crumpled heap about 10 feet away from his original location. He wasn't moving. Matthew was vehemently denying what he had done, but we all knew the truth. I calmly (as calmly as I could anyway) sent him home. I looked closely at the bird and saw he was breathing... barely.

I gently picked him up and yet again, put him back in his nest. The next morning, I awoke again to Ethan reporting that he could hear the bird tweeting loudly outside his window.

Then came the surprise. We finally saw his mother. She was in the tree. We watched her for most of the day. She was flying in and out of the tree, most of the time with worms in her mouth. Although I wondered where in the world "Momma Bird" had been, it was a relief knowing the bird was going to live and that she was there to protect him. "I told Ethan: always remember: God and his momma can take care of him the best." We couldn't believe what happened next.

The following morning that dang bird was back on the ground! I absolutely refused to put that bird in the nest another time. Ethan was crying, but I just refused to do it. I couldn't for the life of me understand why that mother wasn't taking better care of her baby! WHY would she allow that bird to get out of the nest?

Ethan wanted to go over and see the bird. I told him he could, but to my amazement, when he walked over to look it, the mother bird came out of nowhere and flew into Nate's back! She totally dive-bombed him! It didn't hurt Nate, but it did startle him.

A bit confused, he walked back over to me and I told him, "I guess his Mom is still watching over him, huh?" He shook his head, "Yeah."

We watched through our window as the bird hopped around. There was even a scare with the neighbor's mean cat entering the picture, but "Momma Bird" quickly chased him away. The bird continued to hop around our yard for the next week. We walked outside every day to see his progress. Every time we got close to him, his mother was ever watchful, squawking at us, warning us to stay away, which we did. Every day he got a little bigger, until the day arrived when the hopping turned into flying. "Junior" had finally spread his wings and flown. That's when I had a lightbulb moment. All of a sudden, I understood HOW to do the FlyLady routines, and although the turmoil in my family was a big motivator, my own "Why" had not yet been nailed down.

Here I was feeling sorry for the bird and continually putting him back in the nest. It occurred to me, the mother was kicking the bird out of the nest because that's the only way the bird could grow! The mother wasn't being cruel. She was helping her baby develop. Although the baby was out of the nest, she was still there to care for her.

What really stuck out was that every day as I watched the developing bird hop around our yard, there was the sound of birds chirping in our trees. It's like they were cheering that baby on saying, "Come on! You can do it! Fly! Fly! FLY!" And after hopping, flopping, trying, and failing over and over again, the baby did it. He flew!

The lesson was all too clear to me. I wanted to fly. I wanted to fly in my housework, home life, finances and relationships; but up until now I had just been hopping and limping along looking for somebody to place me back into the comfort of my nest, as if that would help. I was longing for the nest, but getting out of my comfort zone and trying, failing and trying again was making me stronger.

I think it was a "God Breeze" designed to blow me out of the nest so I could learn to fly. I read in FlyLady's book that "FLYing" stands for "Finally Loving Yourself."

That was a big key that was missing for me: I had not loved myself! But if that baby bird had been willing to get out of the nest, take a few kicks, continue hopping and never give up so he could eventually FLY, then I could too. He didn't give up just because he failed a time or two. He eventually flew and when he did fly it wasn't perfect, but he was still flying. Momma Bird didn't expect perfection, just effort. As the FlyLady says, "Housework done incorrectly still blesses your family."

I now had my own reason WHY I was going to succeed. Excuses, procrastination, and perfectionism were not going to stop me. I was going to tackle my monthly focus and my Baby Steps with a new resolve.

I walked outside on our front porch and sipped my coffee. As I listened to the birds chirping and singing, their song called to me "FLY! FLY!"

And I could feel my wings spreading. I was going to FLY!

I've been reading this diary for nine days now. My husband has been watching me reading this at all hours of the day. "Courtney? What is that old book you're reading?" he asked.

I told him it was a diary I found in a trunk. He gave me an odd look then walked away. Maybe he would understand it later.

Out of everything I had read, this part of the diary really hit me. I had one of those "God Breezes" Gina was talking about. I could see myself as that bird. God was kicking me out of the nest. I kept trying to crawl back into the nest. I wanted to be in a comfortable, safe place, but that really wasn't God's plan for me. I wasn't made to stay in the nest. I was made to FLY!

In fact, I said that out loud to myself several times. "I was made to FLY! I was MADE to FLY! I WAS MADE TO FLY!" It felt so good to say it! It made me think of Dorothy in The Wizard of Oz clicking her heels together and saying, "There's no place like home." Oh, how I wanted that to be true... There's no place like home.

Chapter 9
Out of Shape

Dear Diary,

The day started with my newfound commitment to "FLY" like that bird. I got up and did my morning routine. Doing my before bedtime routine at night really made my mornings go so much easier. The 31 Baby Steps kept me right on track. In fact, many of them were becoming second nature to me.

Decluttering was making a big difference in my house. I could see real results. Even Brittany commented on the kitchen looking better. She didn't say it to me, but I heard her say it to Ethan.

I noticed I needed some more trash bags to keep up with my new routines, plus, we needed some groceries. I walked out to the front yard to see Ethan playing. He has so much energy. He wanted me to play with him so I ran around, playing tag with him... for about two minutes. Then I couldn't breathe.

Believe it or not, I actually ran cross country in high school and now I couldn't run one lap around my front yard! I was that out of shape!

Sure, I gained weight with the kids. Who doesn't? I know lots of women who struggle with getting that weight off. I just figured I was one of those people who was stuck with the baby fat. It definitely wasn't for lack of trying. I had tried every diet known to man. I would get sucked in by those weight-loss infomercials when Dan wasn't around. Sometimes I would watch the same one over and over just to feel better about purchasing it, but then I really would not do anything with it.

I was sitting on the front porch steps, catching my breath, trying to remember why I gained all this weight, when Ethan came running up to me and asked, "Hey, Mom! Can we go to Burger Barn for lunch like we did last week?" It was at that moment that it hit me: I am a spontaneous eater. I had no plans for breakfast, I had no plans for lunch, and I really had no plans for dinner either.

Eating for us was spontaneous and based solely on what mood we were in when we were 5 minutes away from eating time. But my life was so busy, what could I do about it? As luck would have it, the email from FlyLady this morning was about Menu Planning. I remembered reading something in her book about it. This email was about spontaneous eating leading to an unhealthy lifestyle. It's like FlyLady was a "fly" on my wall with special insight into my life! Whoa-oh!

I read the email knowing it was going to hit me between the eyes, but then again, maybe that's what I needed. The email had a testimonial from a "FlyBaby" (as they are called) who said she was overweight and that 90% of her meals came from eating out. The result was an unhealthy diet, a splintered family, and a busted budget.

I guess I hadn't thought of all that. The email said, "Of course we know fast food is unhealthy." I guess that was true unless I got a salad or something. But later on in the email she said she found out that some fast-food salads are worse for you than a hamburger! I never knew that.

She also said whenever her family had fast food, they tended to eat it and all go their separate ways. They didn't sit around the table as a family and talk. Instead, they watched TV. Fast food made for no conversation or true family time. I started thinking about the times our family actually just sat around and talked. Other than major holidays we really didn't do that. In fact, during the times we were around the table, the TV was usually on and nobody was paying any attention to anybody else.

The testimonial continued to talk about how they were in the hole every month with their finances and how shocked they were when they actually added up how much money they were spending eating out. They said it was nearly a <u>third</u> of their monthly budget! I was afraid to even look at how much money we were spending.

I honestly hadn't thought about how many other things in my life were affected by simply not planning out my meals, but as I evaluated my life, I could see myself in this lady's email. She continued explaining the difference Menu Planning had made in their life. She let the whole family participate.

They started making some healthier choices and they actually had fun doing it. Because they all participated in the process, they became more excited about eating together. Their conversations around the dinner table became fun and fulfilling times. They bonded in a way they had never previously done. They became a loving family.

And they cut their food expenses by half! Half! That was a huge cut! But the best part was the weight she had lost. Simply by planning out her meals and sticking with it, she had lost 20 pounds in two months! She thanked FlyLady for saving her wallet, her waistline, and her family time. It had made a huge difference.

The habit for this month was Menu Planning. I was convinced: I had to start planning out menus for the family. I pretty much knew Brittany and Dan wouldn't participate, at least not at first. Ethan, of course, was willing to help. The only problem was, he wanted pizza every night! Karly, on the other hand, wanted some other choices. She was tired of eating out. When I told them we were going to eat a home-cooked meal every night, Ethan innocently asked, "Is Nana coming over to cook it?"

The truth hurt. I hadn't cooked a meal in a long, long time. I politely answered, "No, Ethan. I'm going to cook it."

"All right!!!" Ethan exclaimed. Oh, how I loved my little cheerleader. He always believed in me, even when I didn't believe in myself.

In Sink Reflections, I read about Menu Planning. She said, "Part of FLYing is knowing what's for supper." Well, I was definitely committed to FLY and I wasn't stopping now. It did seem like a great way to control my eating. My biggest problem was impulse eating. I ate what I felt like, when I felt like it, because I really had no plan. In fact, I normally didn't even think about what to fix for dinner until about... well, I guess I didn't think about it until everybody started asking me what was for dinner.

Then I would usually run through the closest drive thru. It was quick and easy. It seemed to be a good solution for everybody, but now my body was suffering from years of food abuse. I knew the food was bad for us, but the convenience of it seemed to make it a habit.

Menu Planning could also kill two birds with one stone. Not only would it help us eat in a healthy way, but if I could get these meals planned out like FlyLady said, I could conceivably get my family to eat together at the dining room table every night. That would have to help our family communication, not to mention the overall tension in the house.

I called Susan to ask her about it. She was headed out to the grocery store anyway so we decided to go together. She helped me *pick out real food. Talking with her helped me confirm my commitment to follow through with the meal plans. Admittedly, I'm not that great of a cook, but the bottom line was: I was willing to try and learn.*

I can't say that every choice Susan was telling me to make was my favorite, but she gave me four little rules she had read in FlyLady's and Leanne Ely's book, Body Clutter, for picking out food: 1. Is it going to bless my body? 2. Does it fit into my healthy way of eating? 3. Is the taste worthy enough to go into my body? 4. Why do I want to eat it?

The last one was the toughest for me to answer. Honestly, I had read books and bought countless "Lose weight" products that were "guaranteed" to help me lose my flab, but I hadn't followed through. I suppose the WHY was more important than the HOW. As I said, I eat for comfort from stress and heartache. With the last six months of my life, it's no wonder I've gained so much weight. I basically admitted I didn't eat to bless my body. I ate based on how I felt at the moment. I realized that I was an emotional eater.

Body Clutter addressed "HALT," which stands for "Hungry, Angry, Lonely or Tired." We should think about these things before we stuff our faces, to make sure the need is really hunger. This helped me think about my motivation. We walked through the grocery store picking out things. I told her how I didn't relish the thought of fixing two meals a night.

"What do you mean?" Susan asked.

"I mean a meal for me and a meal for the kids," I replied.

Susan just looked at me for a minute before she gently said, "Gina, you're going to all this trouble to plan the meals and get healthy, don't you think your family deserves to be healthy too?" I got what she was saying. "You only have to fix one meal a night. Let your family share in this healthy lifestyle."

I paid for the food. Truth be told, I could've used that money for other things, but that's a story for another day. We were walking out to my car to load the grocery bags when a flood of emotions began to drown me. All I could hear was Brittany and Dan's voices, "You've never followed through with anything! How is this different from every other time?" And now I had just spent a truckload of money on it. I began to tear up a little bit. I was worried that I would fail again.

Susan asked, "What's wrong?"

"I just don't know if I can do this, Susan. I've tried everything before. Brittany told me not too long ago that I always start things and never finish them. Weight loss is so hard and my metabolism is slow, and besides, I know how much I LOVE chocolate. I just don't think that I can do it."

Susan didn't say anything, which concerned me a bit. She just helped me load the groceries in the back of the car and pushed the cart into a collection bin. Then she got into the passenger seat of my car and said, "Let's talk about something for a minute."

"Gina, let's talk about <u>why</u> you want to do this. I can show you what I ate to lose my weight, but I can't give you the motivation to actually follow through. You have to want it. And... I mean this with all my heart... you have to quit making excuses. I did the same thing. I had every excuse as to why I couldn't lose weight, but here is the truth: I didn't love myself. Remember "FLYing?" It means "Finally Loving Yourself?"

I nodded my head.

"Gina, it's time to love yourself. You can't take care of your family and your house until you love yourself. You've made SO much progress. I know you can do this, too. You just have to do it like you did your house: Baby Steps. But you can't do it if you make excuses. You have to eliminate them from your life. They're holding you back just like they held me back. Once I realized I was in charge of my life, things started to change for the better. It wasn't magic but I started making progress.

"Take one step at a time. It worked for you with your house and it will work here. If you're like me, you try to do too much at once which causes you to burn out. Don't do that. Let's just start with this plan." We planned out a month's worth of menus. Knowing what I was going to cook was half the battle.

"Can I still keep up my 31 Baby Steps with my house?" I asked.

"Yes you can! And with a little consistency, it will get easier each day," Susan replied, "But just remember: your focus for this month is fixing those meals for your family. One thing that I did that made dinner seem special was to put some candles on the table."

I paused for a minute, then summoned my courage and replied, "Ok. I will." We talked for a few more minutes about the meals and then it was time to head home and take the second step... cook!

I was really thinking about all she had said. She was exactly right. I had used excuses all my life. There was always a reason why I couldn't or didn't do something. I didn't like hearing it, but I knew Susan had been where I was before and that made it easier to hear. I had to eliminate the excuses from my life if I was going to truly change. NOW was the time.

I drove home, got out my menu plan, and went to work on the evening meal. I remember reading that FlyLady suggested when you cook, to clean up as you go, to keep the clutter down, which is exactly what I did. I filled up the sink with hot soapy water and cleaned up as I cooked.

By the time 5:30 rolled around, I had the meal ready. It was a bit funny seeing the kids' reactions to me cooking dinner. To Ethan and Karly, who had helped me plan it out, it seemed like a new adventure, but it was a different feeling from Brittany. Dan walked in at 5:35. It was awkward, but I resolved that this night would be about having a pleasant evening around the dinner table... and we did.

All Dan said when he saw the table setting was, "Wow." Not an exuberant "Wow." It was just a stunned "Wow," but it was something more than I had before. We sat down, Ethan prayed, and then we ate. It was actually good, too! Ok, it was only salad and spaghetti, which is difficult to mess up, but the candles on the table gave it the feel of an intimate, Italian restaurant.

During dinner, Karly and Ethan told stories of their day. I waited to see if Dan would talk about his day, but he didn't. Ethan, the comedian of the family, kept us laughing. Even Brittany smiled at a few of his stories. This was actually working! And this meal cost us about a quarter of what eating out normally cost! I have to admit: I was proud of myself!

That night after I cleaned up (it was much easier than usual because, like FlyLady said, there wasn't a huge mess to clean up after dinner.) I had a feeling of satisfaction. I had accomplished a nice meal for my family, we had a great time eating it together around the table, and I felt satisfied without my usual gorging of ice cream and chocolate. It was progress in the right direction. I mean, it was a Baby Step in the right direction.

I went to bed happy and content, with my sink shining.

I closed the diary and thought to myself, "All this started with just shining a sink??" How could shining a sink accomplish so much? Then again, what did I know? I walked into my kitchen and it was a disaster. Dirty dishes everywhere full of half eaten food, crumbs on the floor, stains on the countertops, and no clean dishes in the cabinets. I couldn't really say anything. It was as if I had never really seen it until now.

That's when the phone rang. It was Bobby, my husband, informing me that his mother would arrive in about two hours. He apologized for not telling me sooner but he got busy at work. My priorities were no longer just shining a sink. I had to have this house in order and <u>fast</u>. Time for Stash and Dash! I began running around the house and picking up whatever I could off the floor and throwing it wherever I could.

The trick was finding the appropriate places. Some of them were obvious. Of course the dirty dishes and Tupperware would go in the oven. Dirty laundry? In the showers, as usual. When it came to magazines, old papers, and boxes, I had to get a little creative. The magazines went under the couch; no chance of them being found there. I had to slide around the magazines that were already there from the last time I did this, but thankfully there was still room. I don't exactly remember where I put the boxes. I was a cleaning maniac! Before I knew it, everything in the house was presentable! It actually looked good.

Now I had to remember where I put the vacuum cleaner last. Oh! That's right. I put it in the laundry room on top of the washer and dryer so I could get to it. Great! Once the floors were vacuumed they didn't look half bad. I was ready for my mother-in-law.

And just in time. As I threw the vacuum back where I got it from in the laundry room, the doorbell rang.

As she walked in the door I immediately noticed her face. It had a forced smile then a look of surprise as she said, "Wow. The house looks nice." As if that were some big shock! I always clean when she's coming! I wonder if Bobby had been complaining about me to his mother again.

She walked around the house looking like a drill sergeant with white gloves on an inspection tour. My heart began to beat faster. The kids came into the room to interrupt the "inspection." They ran up to "Grammy" and she gave them a hug.

She commented, "Look how skinny! Doesn't your mommy ever feed you?"

I bit my tongue. Then my heart skipped another beat. I realized I had nothing for dinner. In a panic I thought, "I can't leave the house! She'll snoop around and find everything!" I thought about taking her with me, but it would be worse to let her see my car.

I knew I could get back and forth from the restaurant in about 30 minutes if I called ahead. I told them I would be back soon and to take "Grammy" to the neighborhood park to play. It sounded like a pretty good cover story. I hopped in the car. I could call the restaurant from the car. At least I knew my cell phone was charged. That would have actually mattered if I had not left it at home. I got to the restaurant and ran inside to place my to-go order.

When I got home with the food an hour later, everybody, including Bobby, was home. I wondered if I had been discovered or not. The kids approached me with the wonderful announcement, "Grammy needs toilet paper. We can't find any in the house!"

Oh, no! People are looking around my house for something!! I frantically ran upstairs. There was my mother-in-law about to go in the bedroom. "It's ok!" I exclaimed. "I can find it for you!" I ran ahead of her into my bedroom and found half of what was probably the last roll in the house and slipped out the door to hand it to her. She had gone downstairs. As I watched her open the downstairs linen closet, it occurred to me where I had placed all those boxes. They fell in a cascade on her along with a waterfall of laundry and toys. I was mortified.

"Oh! I'm so sorry!" She just gave me that same forced smile as my husband and kids ran around the corner to see what the commotion was. She shot a look at her son, my husband, which was an all too clear expression of great displeasure. It wasn't the first time I'd seen that look.

It was about then that my daughter offered, "I'm sorry, Grammy. Usually we throw that stuff in the upstairs closet."

It was my turn to shoot the look and tell my daughter that she was clearly NOT helping.

My husband, sensing the tension, said, "Why don't we get that dinner on the table." He helped the kids out of the room, along with Grammy.

After the long wait, the trip home, and the toilet paper search, the food had gotten cold. No problem. I'd just heat it up in the oven. I set the preheat timer. In about 10 minutes my house was filled with smoke. If anyone is wondering, Tupperware begins melting at about 230 degrees and smells like a fire at a Goodyear tire plant. It's also extremely hard to clean out of an oven (even one with a "self-cleaning" feature). I think the fire alarms in the house were similar to the shot heard 'round the world.

Everyone informed me they couldn't eat in a house that smelled that bad. So… it was back out to eat. I threw the other food in the refrigerator for later and told everyone to load up in the car. Grammy said, "You're not going to take these kids out in public looking like that. Aren't they going to clean up?"

Sheepishly I replied, "Of course." The look on my face was enough to warn my daughter not to give any further commentary. I told the kids quietly to run upstairs, clean up, and get ready as quickly as they could.

Grammy sat down on the living room couch and said, "I'll just wait here while you go clean up too." With a forced smile, I handed her the remote control to the TV (to avoid shoving it in her mouth) and told her to make herself at home. I ran upstairs to clean up and change clothes. My daughter met me coming out of the shower in my husband's soaking wet suit. "Look mom! I can wear daddy's clothes!"

"What on Earth? Why are you wearing them in the shower?" I cried.

"They were already in there! I just figured I would help you wash them."

I removed the "dry clean only" suit from my daughter and helped her get dressed. We left for dinner in my messy car as my mother-in-law proceeded to make snide comments about the condition of my car as well as make light of the events of the day by teasing me about every detail. Thankfully, our dinner was uneventful.

Finally we were back home and as soon as we walked in the door, Grammy announced, "Well after the day I've had I need a long, hot bath." Bobby stepped in and told her to go upstairs and help herself. I was too ashamed to even speak.

I went upstairs with the kids and told them to brush their teeth, when my youngest came out and told me she wasn't brushing her teeth tonight. When I told her I was NOT in the mood to argue with her about it, she announced, "But Mommy, the water isn't working."

What?? I ran into the kid's bathroom and sure enough, the water was not working. Oh my gosh!! I had forgotten to pay the stinking bill... again. I ran out to tell Bobby but he was already in the hallway talking to his mother who was in her housecoat glaring at me. She glibly looked at Bobby and clearly for my benefit and said, "So I guess I'll just go to bed filthy, Bobby. Hopefully the electricity will remain on. I'd hate for us all to freeze to death." And with that she shut her door.

Bobby turned to look at me. I apologized for forgetting. I don't know why I'm such an airhead! He just turned to me and said, "We'll go first thing in the morning and pay the bill." It wasn't like we didn't have the money. We just didn't have a reliable person to pay the bill: me. Bobby kindly kissed me on the head and walked into our bedroom and shut the door without saying another word.

As I walked down the stairs, tears of humiliation began to creep from my eyes. I had been caught and my world came crumbling down around me all because of MY lack of planning. I had ten thousand reasons why I had never kept up with the housework or accomplished important things I needed to do, but when it came down to it, they were all simply excuses. Like Gina in the diary, I knew my life had to change. And if I was going to truly change, then I had to take responsibility for my own life. Nobody was going to do it for me. Besides, if Gina and all these other million plus "FlyBabies" could do it, why couldn't I?

After a "cooling off period" I went back upstairs, climbed into bed, and tossed and turned. The events of the day and the diary were preying on my mind. I thought, "Tomorrow is going to be a different day." Then it hit me. Tomorrow never arrives for me. I began to feel the pain of my current situation and I suddenly became mad at my excuses. I realized there was only one way to combat these excuses and procrastination. And that is to do something… NOW. I had to do something… but that something had to be the RIGHT something.

It seemed like I was always busy doing anything except what I really needed to do. Then it hit me. That's the worst kind of procrastination there is: doing everything except what you need to be doing. It's also the most dangerous kind of procrastination because we can confuse being busy with accomplishing something. I had to do the right kind of actions, just like the woman in the diary, Gina, took the right actions.

At 11:30 PM I quietly went back downstairs… and I cleaned my sink.

As I scrubbed and cleaned, tears of humiliation turned into a smile of accomplishment. I had taken my first Baby Step on my new journey. In spite of everything that had happened, I could say one thing for sure about today:

Sink shiny and clean: check.

The next morning, after the kids got to school, I picked up the diary and read the next entry from Gina:

Dear Diary,

The time came for Susan and I to have our conversation about the monthly habit for December. She started our conversation with a very odd question.

Chapter 10
Control Journal & Pampering Yourself

"Have you ever flown on an airplane?" Susan asked as though I had missed the beginning of our conversation somehow.

"Yes..." I replied, thinking it was such a random, odd question.

"Ok," Susan said, "How much time do you actually spend pampering yourself?"

"It depends on what you mean by pampering," I replied.

"I mean," Susan explained, "How much time do you spend taking care of yourself? Your hair? Your clothes? Bubble baths? Going to a spa?"

I laughed, "I don't have time to do those things! Besides, I'd feel guilty if I did. My family and my house demand my time."

"But that's my point, Gina," Susan continued, "You HAVE to make time. Remember what FLYing stands for... 'Finally Loving YOURSELF.' You're not equipped to love your family until you first take care of yourself. That's why I asked you about flying on an airplane. When they give you the safety talk, they tell you that if the oxygen mask drops, always place it on yourself BEFORE you help someone else. If you don't take care of yourself, you won't be able to take care of anybody else."

"I see your point. What do you suggest as a starting point?"

Susan replied, "You told me you've been getting up and getting dressed to your lace up shoes as part of your morning routine, right?"

"Yes"

"And you're fixing your hair."

"Brushing it," I clarified, "I'm not sure I know how to fix it anymore."

"I understand, Gina. When it's been a while since we've truly taken care of ourselves, we can tend to forget how to do it. The monthly focus for December is pampering yourself and it's high time you did it. I have something for you and I don't want you to argue with me about it. It's a gift and I want you to take it. It's a gift certificate to a day spa."

I immediately interjected, "I can't take that! Besides, I don't have a day to go."

"You do have time. You just have to make a little time. Besides, I already set appointments for you."

"When?"

"Today."

"TODAY?" I exclaimed. "I can't go today! Who is going to pick my kids up from school?"

"I will. I will take care of it. You just call the school and tell them. Your kids can come to my house and you can pick them up. You'll still be done before dinner AND I'm fixing dinner for you tonight. Don't worry; it's on your menu. I told you I didn't want you to argue with me! Accept it as a gift. Please? For me?"

I begrudgingly agreed. What was I going to say? No? After all she had done for me?

"And one last thing," Susan continued. "Promise me you will not think about anything today other than YOUR enjoyment and you won't feel guilty about it. Promise?"

What else could I do? I promised her and I went. Ok, it was great. No. It was HEAVENLY. I couldn't remember the last time I had felt this good. Inevitably guilt started creeping in for being there, but I remembered my promise to Susan and focused on how good it felt. I got a massage, a facial, a pedicure, AND a makeover. This really was "the works!" I left the spa feeling like a new woman.

When I arrived at Susan's house to pick up the kids, their reaction to me was nothing short of wonderful. Karly smiled at me. Ethan told me how beautiful I looked (although he usually did). Susan smiled and told me, "This was the person I always knew was inside you." It felt so good. Susan gave me the wonderful dinner she had prepared for us and I took it home to warm it up.

I guess the best news would have to be when Dan got home. We were sitting around the dinner table, eating and talking, when I noticed Dan looking at me. Ok, he didn't just look, he stared... and even smiled. Then I finally heard some words I hadn't heard in months... scratch that, YEARS. He looked at me and said, "You look so pretty." I wanted to go in another room and cry tears of joy, but I just smiled and said, "Thank you, Dan."

The next day I couldn't wait to tell Susan all about it. We laughed together over this victory. The momentum in my life, which for the last 20 years had been going in the wrong direction, was starting to swing the other way. The value of fixing myself up every day wasn't for anyone else, but for my OWN self esteem.

I was starting to have trouble putting everything together: the 31 Baby Steps, the monthly habit, morning and evening routines,

97

and decluttering. I was enjoying the process by now and things were starting to feel more routine, but I felt like I did when I was a kid putting together a puzzle.

My mom used to buy these 1000 piece puzzles. You would have to spend hours finding the edges and figuring out how they went together. Then you would find pieces of the pictures and you could complete smaller pictures inside the larger puzzle, but connecting them all together was hard. That's EXACTLY how I was feeling.

I felt as if I had put together a few pictures of my life's puzzle, even finding some of the edges, but connecting all the pieces to form the big picture just wasn't happening. I was slipping on some things, forgetting others all together. I had to come up with a way that helped me remember it all. I explained this to Susan and she said, "You mean you need a Control Journal."

I remembered reading about it in <u>Sink Reflections</u> and in the Baby Steps, but I had never attempted to put it together. I wasn't very sure where to start so I went back to the FlyLady website for instructions. Naturally, she had a complete materials list. I made my list and called Susan to ask about all the different parts.

"You don't need to do it all at once, Gina. Remember: BABY STEPS! I'll go to the store with you and get the necessities, but just realize, this will take you a while to complete. Actually, you don't ever really complete it. It's always a work in progress. I'll bring mine with me."

We met at my favorite place to shop, the office supply store. Susan showed me her journal. It was a three-ring binder. Inside was paper in sheet protectors and there were tabs dividing the sections. On the inside pockets was a pen and a dry erase marker.

"Come on, girl," Susan said, "This won't take long."

First we had to find a 1½ inch three-ring binder notebook. It had to be one I liked and it had to look good in my kitchen. I found one with a color I liked and it had a clear plastic sleeve in the front so I could put a picture in it if I wanted. Then we found some sheet protectors. I wanted to buy 100 but Susan made me start with 20 so I didn't get overwhelmed. Next we found some colored paper, pens, and a small packet of dry erase markers. Last of all we found the blank dividers to go between the sections. That was it. Susan assured me that was plenty to get started.

When I got home, I wrote out my 31 Baby Steps on one page, my morning and evening routines on one, my monthly focus on another, and my menu plans on another. With the tabs, they were always easy to find. Every time I added something else to my schedule or routines, I simply added it to the notebook. I placed the colored sheets in my sheet protectors. This enabled me to mark off a task with the dry erase marker when I had finished it. It really gave me peace of mind checking it off my list. I no longer had to worry about whether or not I had forgotten some important task. It was fun checking things off and seeing my progress.

Every day I would refer to this journal. It really helped my tasks go so much smoother and even faster because I wasn't spending time trying to remember things or round up all my previously posted "sticky note reminders." It was all in one place now! Woohoo!

As the month rolled on, I did go back to the store and add some more pages. They included emergency information, extra to do lists, even a few (and I mean FEW) of my favorite recipes. Susan was right; it was a work in progress. And the wonderful part was, it was my own design. MY Control Journal (although the contents were similar) was different from Susan's. But just like

FlyLady said, I made it my own. I was learning to adapt the routines to fit my family's needs and mine.

Even in the middle of working on my Control Journal, I also kept up with my monthly emphasis for December: Pampering myself. I made it a point every day to get up, fix my hair and makeup (I got some GREAT tips from the stylists and artists at the spa-- it wasn't nearly as hard as I thought it was) and even dress nicer.

I was still losing weight, too! I was up to 19 pounds lost and SO proud! I still had a long way to go, but it was progress. Go ME! I got rid of some of those frumpy clothes and bought a few nicer casual pieces that complimented me. It was really working, too, because Dan commented on how nice I looked in my new clothes.

Pampering myself this month has made a major difference in my life. We're in the middle of our Christmas break now. The kids are spending the night away and Dan and I are going to enjoy a romantic evening together, but first, I'm going to have a nice, hot bubble bath.

Merry Christmas to me.

And a Happy New Year is on the way...

I closed the diary thinking how wonderful it would be to just go to a spa for a day. I knew we couldn't afford it though, and there wasn't a "Susan" in my life to give it to me. I couldn't get away from the kids either. It all sounded great on paper, but applying it all to my busy life wasn't going to work.

Besides, looking at my house, I definitely didn't feel right about leaving this mess to pamper myself. I didn't really deserve it. I was thinking it was something that needed to be earned. I suppose I could put a spa day on my credit card that Bobby didn't know about, but I felt like I was already in enough trouble there without adding to it.

I signed up for the FlyLady email list. They really give you a lot of information. I found one email about pampering yourself. It was the monthly habit for December, but since I was just starting out, could I really do it? The email said one lady pampered herself by taking a bubble bath every day. I could do that! Another email said she would curl up in a chair and read a wonderful book. For me, a 30-minute nap in the afternoon would pamper me. And that's free too!

I was able to find a 30-minute window on Saturday when Bobby took the kids to the store. I lay down and woke up to the kids in my face. I thought they had taken the shortest trip ever to the store. I actually had slept for an hour and a half. I guess I was catching up from my late night sink shining.

I rolled out of bed and felt better. That night I also took a bubble bath. It was heavenly. I noticed the next several days I was much more productive. Perhaps there was something to this "taking care of myself" that helped me take better care of my family and house. I still had a very long way to go though.

Gina had accomplished so much. I was still at square one. I had shined my sink. I even planned out a few meals for my family. But I had not really done anything since then. I kind of felt like Gina when she said she started things she didn't finish.

Then I noticed the saying at the bottom of the FlyLady emails. "You are not behind! I don't want you to try to catch up; I just want you to jump in where you are. O.K.?" I needed to be reminded of it often. I needed to believe in myself more. I needed to start over... yet again. That's ok... I'll jump in where they are.

Chapter 11
New Year, New Beginnings, New Me

A new year... FlyLady's words rang in my head... "What you think about, you bring about."

Some of the things I thought about myself were:

"You look ugly!"
"You're fat!"
"You're lazy."
"They might can do this, but there's no way you can!"
"You NEVER follow through!"
"You're a loser!"
"Why can't you be more like _____?"

I was definitely going to need to change this. I had lunch cooking in a slow cooker, so the family enjoyed a Sunday lunch around the dinner table, then I decided to curl up with the diary and see how Gina started her year. It was remarkably similar:

Dear Diary,

As I welcome this New Year, there are many things I want to say "goodbye" to. I've decided to say goodbye to the old Gina. I didn't really like her anyway and I certainly didn't love her. She didn't follow through with her commitments. She had terrible relationships with her friends and family. Her life was in a constant state of CHAOS. So today: I am saying goodbye to that old way of life.

Now, I have to admit, as soon as I made this decision, all the negative voices in my mind began to attack me saying, "You haven't changed a bit!" These are the same voices I have heard all my life. I could hear it in the voices of my parents telling me what an airhead I was. I could hear it in the voices of some of my teachers who belittled me. I could hear it in hundreds of people throughout the years who told me negative things with their sideways looks, their words, and their actions. Everything screamed at me, you can't, you can't.

All those voices over the years had turned into one condemning voice… and it had become my voice. I was mean to myself. I have trouble trusting people and forgiving them. I've had to deal with forgiveness issues in the past. The bottom line is, the person I've had the most trouble forgiving is myself. But today, here and now, I am going to start forgiving myself of my past failures. I am choosing to daily release the pain of the past, teach myself to live in the present, and to find joy in all I do. I am DONE with my old ways and the old me. They're gone. I don't care what people say. I don't care what I've been. I'm becoming a new me!

In order to boost my growth by reminding myself of this, I've posted some notes on my bathroom mirror.

"I am learning to love myself each day."

"I have an exciting new future ahead of me!"

"I do not over-commit myself. I can say no and not feel guilty about it."

"I follow through with my commitments."

"My house is becoming a home."

"My home is a peaceful place to be."

"I'm improving my relationships with my friends and my family."

"My husband and I are growing closer to each other than ever before."

"I am concentrating on becoming a better manager at home."

"I am becoming organized and enjoy the peace it affords me."

"I am becoming the person I've always admired."

I've started reading the affirmations to myself every morning and it is really making a difference in my life! I realize I'm actually starting to become what I'm reading, which excites me. I've made a commitment to read these every morning while I'm getting ready. It only takes a minute and I feel SO good when I'm done! Sometimes if there is one that stands out, I grab that sticky note and take it with me for the day to remind myself to work on it.

I'm off to clean my sink and do my routines. Today I'm doing my routines with a BIG smile on my face because I know what great rewards await me for showing up and taking one Baby Step.

Reading Gina's issues with forgiving herself struck home with me. I've heard those same negative voices in my head and they are holding me back. I knew I would have to explore this some more.

I went back and reread Gina's affirmations. I felt silly reading them at first, then silliness changed to conviction. I really wanted all these things in my life. My mind was in a war though. Every time I read them my mind would tell me how unworthy I was. I never realized how much I had been "brain damaged" from my past. The great news was that it was operable.

I wrote out just three affirmations for me:

"I love myself."

"I am highly capable."

"Baby Steps will get me there."

I decided to write them on a sheet of paper and keep it with me today. By the end of the day I was glad I did.

FlyLady's monthly focus for January is cleaning your sink. I decided to start there. I followed the exact plan that Gina did in the diary. It didn't take me long to get my sink sparkling clean. When I was finished I read my affirmations. The combination of my clean sink and these positive words helped me start to believe that what I was saying really was true.

I decided to start the 31 Baby Steps, too. I was ready to jump in. I was trying to be careful not to bite off more than I could chew, but I was so motivated and excited, it was hard not to go overboard.

I looked over the Baby Steps. They really didn't seem that bad. After all, "I was learning and growing and becoming the person I always wanted to be!" How could it be bad?

I continued my routine for four days, my husband even commented on my new energy. He seemed so pleased with me. The kids had to go back to school on day five. Everything was feeling so fresh and new. And then I had a very close call.

I had forgotten to go out and get the mail that day. I normally always get it but I guess I was so excited about everything that I just forgot to go get it. Bobby picked up the mail and the bill for my secret credit card was in there! I had managed to keep it hidden for eight months.

I only got the card to be able to do a few surprise purchases. You know how it goes? You're checking out at the store and they offer you 15% off if you sign up for the card. I never intended to put that much on it but I was able to make all the minimum payments. It was all for clothes for the kids and other things they needed. It's not like I spent any of it on myself. I was trying to get it down with some extra money I had made, but I just couldn't get that principal down. Then there were the times I forgot to pay it and late fees started piling up and got me into trouble.

I was able to keep Bobby from seeing the bill. He was suspicious but I covered it up. I felt really badly about it, but I just couldn't bring myself to tell him. I knew I would have to tell him someday, but today was not going to be that day. I was so worried that he would lose all trust in me again.

That night as I got ready for bed I came across those affirmations. I just looked at them and started to cry. There was no way I could let any of those words leave my lips. Not on that night. I didn't feel worthy of love. I felt like I had taken a jump backwards in my self-esteem. I didn't sleep well that night.... Guilty conscience.

I went back to my basic routine. Keeping my sink shiny was easy. I was working through the Baby Steps just one day at a time along with my "stinking thinking". One day at a time was doable. Trying to do it all at one time was too big to think about.

Why did I keep that hidden from Bobby? He was very loving and understanding. He wasn't an angry person. The problem was, I knew better. My college major was accounting. I knew how money worked.

I realized this was a control issue with me. I wanted to be in control of my life and have my own say-so. I was a stay-at-home mom and my life never really felt like my own. I felt like a slave to everybody else's schedule. I was constantly helping the kids get to and from their school and other activities. I spent the rest of the time cleaning the house. Other than last month, I didn't take any time out for me. I guess having my own credit card made me feel like there was one thing in my life I was actually in control of.

It still didn't justify it, but at least I understood myself a little bit better. After cleaning up from dinner, I sat down to read my affirmations that I couldn't bring myself to do in the morning. I read over them again:

"I love myself."

"I am highly capable."

"Baby Steps will get me there."

I sat there reading those to myself and after everybody finally went to bed, I stayed downstairs and actually read them out loud.

The power of consistently shining my sink really struck home. All these things were Baby Steps. I was starting to understand things about myself that I had never even noticed before. I was actually becoming a new person. Could it be that when I say those things out loud my brain and soul were finding ways to make them actually come true?

Or... was the truth that I really was that person I wanted to be and was just now discovering it? Suddenly a new word had entered my mind: BELIEF.

It was then that this truth hit me: The words coming out of my mouth are what my subconscious BELIEVES. What it believes about me is what I act out. What I act out is what I become and what I truly am.

The affirmations have changed since that night. I have added to them and taken others away. I have refined them to make them more in line with the person I know I can be. I would write them out, but to be honest, they are far too personal to list here. My affirmations gave me the energy and motivation to complete the 31 Baby Steps this month. I'm making progress and that's good enough. I'm doing this for me.

One thing is for sure, though: from that day to this I have never missed another day of doing my daily affirmations. They have proven to be invaluable to me. I realized that change first takes place in our minds. Actions follow thoughts. This was a major key to unlocking many more victories in my life.

Like Gina, I knew that Baby Steps would get me there! **<u>GO ME</u>**!!

Chapter 12
Decluttering for 15 Minutes a Day

It was the first of February. It was time for me to see what Gina was up to.

Dear Diary,

It is so wonderful to walk around my house and not have to step over mounds of boxes and clutter. FlyLady was right. It's amazing how getting rid of things you don't want or need can change everything about your life.

I think back to when I was first starting to declutter and how frustrated I was. I remember when I felt like I wasn't making any progress and wanted to quit that a testimonial would come into my email from FlyLady that was just what I needed to keep me moving in the right direction.

Today was a red letter day in my life. I invited Susan over to my home to treat her to lunch. I know ... how about that? I actually had a guest in my home. That wasn't possible a few short months ago since I was the poster child for "C.H.A.O.S." (Can't Have Anybody Over Syndrome). I was always embarrassed to answer the door for fear of someone seeing the condition I was allowing my children and husband to live in. Now, for the first time... I had somebody IN my house and I had invited them.

After all that Susan had poured into my life, it seemed the least I could do. As soon as she arrived, she told me how proud she was of me for taking this step. She remembered the first time she invited someone over after she decluttered. It was such a huge stepping-stone for her and she knew how much it meant to me.

As she came in the house she was looking around. It made me feel a little self-conscious due to years and years of being ashamed of my house, but Susan put me immediately at ease. Her smile and sweet words of encouragement put a smile on my face and made me realize all the progress I had made.

I invited her to have a seat in the living room. It was funny to think about asking her to do that because just a few short months ago she couldn't have gotten to the living room through the front door because the path was blocked.

Susan sat down on the couch. I know that doesn't sound like a big deal but it used to be filled with laundry and cat hair. She looked at me and said some words I will never forget, "Gina, the house looks absolutely wonderful. You're doing a great job! It took a lot of commitment and a lot of courage to change, but you did it!"

I was jumping up and down on the inside, but on the outside I just beamed as I replied, "Thanks."

She asked, "So how does it feel to have your home in such beautiful order now?"

"It feels great." But there was tentativeness in my voice that told Susan there was more I was feeling.

"But??" Susan inquired.

"You know, it's odd, but I have so much time on my hands now that sometimes I'm not sure what to do with myself." "Who would have thought that having a clean house didn't take all your extra time but gave you more free time than you knew what to do with it?"

"Yeah," Susan said, "I remember something FlyLady said: Having our homes in order would free our time to be what we were meant to be. I didn't understand it until one day I was looking around for something to do: declutter something, organize something, anything, then it hit me, what FlyLady had meant."

"Yes" I smiled, amazed at how well Susan could read me. "I'm finding myself looking for something more to do, but I'm just not sure what that is."

Then Susan asked, "What do you love to do?"

It had been years since I had thought about that. When you're a kid you think about it some, but I hadn't really thought about it since I was so busy with the clutter of my life.

It wasn't until I was in high school and my teacher asked me to teach a class for her. Then one day I realized: I loved teaching. I loved to study and learn about all the details of things and then communicate them to others. I loved the feeling of seeing someone I'm talking to get that "A-ha!" moment when they catch what I'm telling them. There's really nothing like it for me.

I told Susan, "I majored in education in college, but the kids came along and I never finished my degree. I think I would want to go back to school."

"Really?" Susan exclaimed, "I think that would be fantastic! Why don't you look into it?"

"Well, I don't know..."

Susan immediately jumped in, "It's really going to come down to your belief in yourself, Gina. It starts there. Look around you at what you are capable of by doing one small step at a time."

"I know," I weakly replied, "but it's just that I usually don't follow through with things."

Susan interrupted again, "That was the OLD Gina. That was the Gina with the house full of clutter." And then looking around the room Susan observed, "It's quite obvious 'THAT' Gina doesn't live here anymore."

That was a big moment for me. I realized she was right. I had made a change not just in the house but in me, too. I had to let go of what I was and believe in who I am and, more importantly, what I am going to be. I had a confidence that I hadn't previous had and I said, "You know what? I think I will."

We had a great visit, and after Susan left I sat down with this diary to write out what just happened. I really am a different person. I'm going to look at some college information. I'm contacting my old college to get my credits transferred. I'm sure I'm going to catch grief from Dan about this, but I have to do something. I think he'll eventually support it. Especially since he seems to "REALLY" like this new Gina he's living with.

I'm off to my daily routines now. February is decluttering month. I'm glad that I don't have nearly as much to do as I did several months ago. Strange how what wasn't clutter last month because you couldn't part with it, all of a sudden this month is clearly clutter in my life!

I put the diary down and started thinking about what Gina had said. Although there were a few differences, I did see some of myself in what she was saying. I tended to be my own worst enemy.

My house was still cluttered. There were just some things I wasn't willing to let go of; however, the frustration of stepping over things is greater than the desire to keep some of this stuff. I dove in and started decluttering. I was finally able to part with some things, but others I put in a pile to look through again, exactly the way Gina said she did. I had to laugh at myself for it but eventually Baby Steps would take care of that clutter too.

The next day I woke up to a cluttered home and a sore body that was screaming, "What the heck were you thinking yesterday??"

It seems like I remembered reading something similar in the diary. I read about how Gina read <u>Sink Reflections</u> to get suggestions on items to declutter and exactly how to do it.

I got an email from FlyLady that explained a lot about the February habit. I realized that I had been trying to do too much, too quickly. This seemed to be a theme for my life. I get excited about something, jump in, make changes, get tired of it, burn out, and then quit. I've been through that cycle over and over again and not just with the house either.

I looked over my house and felt behind. I was grateful for the saying at the end of every FlyLady email: "You are not behind! I don't want you to try to catch up; I just want you to jump in where we are. O.K.?"

The time had come to jump in and do it in a way that was proven to work for millions of people just like me. I was going to do FlyLady's 15-minute decluttering. This was much harder to do than it sounded. Not from the standpoint of finding enough to do for 15 minutes at a time, but actually stopping! I wanted to keep going, but I stayed within the boundaries set and only did 15 minutes at a time or until I had 27 items to give away, put away, or throw away. This was my first exercise in believing in

FlyLady. Believing that someone had a plan that would work, as long as I didn't quit.

At first I thought this system was in place to torture me, but after a week of doing these 15 minute sessions, I could see the sessions were really more for my benefit. I wasn't as tired as I usually was and I actually began to look forward to getting these done. I had more energy and was ready to dive in each day because I knew it wasn't going to take all day. I was making progress.

The time was fast approaching for me to say goodbye to clutter I knew I didn't need. I decided to donate some of my old clothes to the local battered women's shelter. I even got a tax deduction for them!

At the end of the month, I wish I could say my house looked great like Gina described and I was ready to invite people over, but I'd be lying if I did. The best thing I can say is it looks way better than it did before. I'm happy with that!

Could it be that, like Gina, I am becoming a new person, too? I hope that is the case. I really do hope for that day. One thing I have to say is there is a strange, new feeling and I like it. I hope this blossoms into a belief in myself like Gina has. I decided to remind myself that I was capable and I drew a picture of a blossom on four sticky notes and put them around the house to remind me that I was blossoming into a new person.

Part of believing in myself is loving myself.

Chapter 13
Comfort vs. Change

Dear Diary,

Susan invited me over to her house this afternoon for some tea and girl time. We have grown very close over these last several months and she has become a true mentor to me. As I drove to her house, I was thinking about asking her about the focus for March, "Getting Dressed to Lace Up Shoes".

Who would have thought that the conversation we were about to have would be a turning point for me?

I walked into Susan's house and I was again (as always!) impressed with how comfortable it made me feel. Everything had a place and it was in it. I don't mean that it was perfect or anything like that. But, it felt like it put its arms around me and hugged me. When I walked through my house, it felt more like a kick in the butt. I was trying to put my finger on what it was when Susan said, "Would you like coffee or tea? I have both."

We walked into her kitchen and I couldn't help myself. I glanced at her sink as we passed it. Yep. It was shiny as could be and smiled at me. The countertops looked polished. I sat down at her table that had a beautiful violet sitting in the center of it. There was no mail, no laundry. It's interesting how simple can be so nice. Susan served the tea out of an old iron teapot that had been her grandmother's. I sat there drinking the tea, looking out the kitchen window, watching the birds outside. Even though it was March, it was still fairly cold. I was looking at how beautiful it was and, without really thinking about it, I let out a sigh.

That is what the difference was between Susan's house and mine. In her house, I just felt so... so.... so....

"Peaceful, isn't it?" Susan interrupted.

I smiled, "That's exactly what I was thinking. But I always feel so peaceful when I'm here. I wish I felt that way at my house. Here you seem so at ease. So peaceful. So comfortable."

"That's part of what I want to talk to you about."

I replied, "I figured we were going to talk about getting dressed to lace up shoes."

Susan confirmed, "That's great that you're reading FlyLady's emails." She sipped her tea, then continued, "You know one of the most important things I learned in this journey is about comfort and change."

"Comfort is what I want!" I interjected.

"Becoming comfortable can be a big problem," Susan explained. The puzzled look on my face told her that I wanted to know more, so she continued, "Becoming comfortable with where you are causes you to stop moving forward. Comfort tells you change is bad. When you become too comfortable with where you are, chaos follows. You have to get to a level of discomfort with where you are to move ahead and find peace.

"I first got a bit of comfort in my home when I had accomplished some real results that were noticeable not only to me but also to my family. I had even started feeling better about myself, well, then it happened. I started getting comfortable. I started 'resting on my laurels.' The problem with being comfortable is, very often, you quit doing the things that made you comfortable in the first place. You quit doing your routines. Somehow or another you feel like your small success has earned you the right to stop, but if you

stop you lose the big payoff: Peace. I stopped my routines just for a week and decided I would start back tomorrow. Tomorrow took me about six months. I don't want that to happen to you, like it did to me."

I told her I appreciated her helping me, but she continued, "There's more."

"More?"

"This is the _most_ important part, Gina. It's about change. You've already been willing to change, but there's more coming. It's the nature of life. When a tree ceases to grow and change, it dies. The same thing is true of us. Change is just a part of living."

Very honestly I replied, "I don't like change."

Susan laughed, "My grandmother used to say that the only people who like change are babies in diapers and even they cry while it's happening. Nobody I know likes change, but it's necessary for us to grow, otherwise WE remain babies all our lives. We have to grow and change and mature. And while we always keep our fun, childlike qualities, growing and changing is necessary."

"I'm not sure I will ever like change." I admitted.

At first it can be hard because it's not a part of our normal thinking. We have to stop and think about what we are doing. We have to remind ourselves to do something different. But after a while the change becomes our new routine. We have grown and become stronger and better. Then...."

"...it's time for change again?" I interrupted.

"Exactly," Susan replied, "and then it's time for us to stretch ourselves and grow again. It's a cycle of growth and it's a healthy one."

I sat there thinking for a moment, then with a pensive look, I asked, "What happens if I don't change and remain the same?"

Susan replied, "It's interesting and confusing all at the same time. We can't remain the same, either because we are getting better or we are getting worse. Change is always happening in people's lives. Those who choose not to change miss their true purpose in life. They don't grow. They don't become what they were meant to be. They completely miss their life's purpose and this causes an emptiness in their hearts. They feel a longing that they try to fill with other things: from shopping for new clutter, to everything from alcohol and drugs, to over-volunteering outside the home. This sacrifices their family's happiness as well as their own happiness and only leaves anger.

After a pause, I was able to say, "I kind of wish I hadn't asked now."

"But someday you'll be glad you did. Keep doing your routines. The routines you're doing will lead you into the change and peace you're looking for and someday it will lead you to the true purpose for your life."

"What is your purpose, Susan?"

Leaning in, she whispered, "Helping others," as a big smile crossed her face.

"I really do want to go to the next step in my life, so what's next?"

Susan responded, "Do your routines. This month I want you to do what you've been doing and just add one thing, getting dressed to lace-up shoes."

"I don't like shoes. I prefer slippers, flip-flops, or even better, barefoot."

"But that's exactly what you don't need to do," she continued. "You don't wear slippers and flip-flops to work. When you get dressed to lace up shoes you can't as easily remove them and it subconsciously tells your mind that it is time to work. Flip Flops and bare feet tell your brain that it's fun time. Tell me the first place you think of when you think of wearing flip-flops or going barefoot.

I immediately said, "The beach." I understood what she meant.

"Trust me, FlyLady has helped millions of women from around the world. Remember there is a method to her madness. Change is turning away from what you have always done to something better. Wearing shoes isn't that big a sacrifice to you, but it's a big deal to your brain. It tells your brain this is serious and it's time for you to go to work."

Susan was right. The FlyLady had helped millions of people get control of their clutter and find joy in their life. Wearing shoes wasn't that big of a deal anyway. I would "step" out in faith in the FlyLady way in my lace-up shoes.

Susan continued, "Your attitude will show you if you are making the change or not. I know you may feel it's only necessary when somebody is watching, but you're not doing it for somebody else. You're doing it for YOU. Remember what 'FLYing' stands for. 'Finally Loving YOURSELF.' When you get dressed to lace-up shoes, not only are you ready for work, you are truly loving yourself. It's just part of respecting yourself."

"I want to do this for me!" I replied.

"Great," smiled Susan, "You won't be sorry."

"It seems like such an insignificant thing but I'm willing."

"The journey of a thousand miles begins with a single step," Susan assured.

"I guess that's true."

"This journey is all about taking one Baby Step at a time to arrive at that destination we were just talking about."

We finished our tea and I headed home. I hadn't thought about putting on lace-up shoes as loving myself, but as the next several days went by I realized that putting on those shoes truly did help me feel ready for work. And I found out when I laced up those shoes on my feet, that I really did think and feel differently. Maybe it was just me but I swear I got a lot more done when I had my shoes on!

I started taking better care of myself too and the funny thing was that as an added benefit my feet were looking much better. Those awful looking cracked heels were going away.

I don't know when it started, but, the kids started changing their attitudes too. Although Brittany didn't say anything, her looks told me she noticed the changes in our home. She began speaking to me a little kinder than usual. I was loving it, but I wasn't going to push it with her. I just casually fell into her pace when she wanted to talk and backed off when she seemed distant.

Then it happened. Brittany came in the door from school in tears. At first she just walked in the door and stared at me, crying. I walked up to her, but didn't grab her to hug her. I was going to let her take that initiative. As I got closer though, she fell on me saying, "Oh, mom! We broke up!"

She and her "boyfriend" had been dating for around eight months. I was none too fond of him, but I knew if I said anything it would make her like him even more. I felt horrible for her broken heart, even worse than if it had been mine, but at the same time I was soooo thrilled that he was out of her life. It was hard for me not to turn cartwheels of joy but her tears kept me in check.

We sat down at the kitchen table and she talked and talked. After 30 minutes of crying, she calmed down. She continued to talk and I would interject a question from time to time. She finally talked her way out of the biggest part of her heartache and into realizing that she hadn't been very happy with him for a long time. In the process Brittany and I started to change our relationship.

Hey! This "change" thing isn't nearly as bad as I thought it would be! It definitely has its rewards. I've got to go, Brittany and I are going out to eat and see a movie tonight for Girls Night Out.

I started getting dressed to lace-up shoes every day. And it made a difference in how I felt about working. I dove into that clutter using the FlyLady system and by the end of the month it had really made a huge change in how I felt about working.

I was able to donate more clothes and toys to the battered women's shelter as well as donate some other items to a thrift store and I even found a few items to donate to Habitat for Humanity. They were all glad to get the donations and it felt great to know I was truly helping other people.

I thought about Gina's relationship with her daughter and it made me grateful for my relationships with my kids. I decided I was going to spend more time with them. Dinner and a movie sounded like a great start. I'm going to make that happen tonight too.

I'm so grateful for my family. After reading the next part of the diary, I became even more grateful.

Chapter 14
You Made Your Bed, Now Lie In it

After reading such wonderful progress in Gina's life, I wasn't prepared for what I was about to read:

Dear Diary,

Could this day possibly be any worse?? I'll start at the beginning. It was the end of the month. I was feeling so good about life. I felt ahead of the game because I had been consistently completing most of my routines. They were actually getting easier. As a matter of fact, my house was really looking good. I felt like I was about to move into maintenance mode, rather than my usual mode of operation: disaster relief!

Everything was going just fine. That is until I had to run my errands for the day. I walked outside and was about to get in my car when I noticed the mailman pulling up so I decided to get the mail. The truck pulled off to reveal Debbie, the nosy neighbor, walking toward me. Her sly smile told me there was some juicy piece of gossip she was ready to dish.

"Gina!!" she cried out to me through that irritating, fake smile that you can spot a mile away, you know the one where the edges of the mouth don't curl up; just like a kid at the table right before they spit something out of their mouth.

"Hi, Debbie. I was just picking up my mail and was on the way to the grocery store."

Debbie's smile broadened even more as she said, "That's funny! I was just at the grocery store and you'll never guess who I saw... Dan!"

My mind began to race. I know my face had to look a bit shocked. Dan?? What was Dan doing at the grocery store? He hated going to the grocery store even when I asked him to pick up something. But he was there? And in the middle of the day??

Debbie, reading my face, continued, "Oh, he wasn't IN the grocery store. He was going into the restaurant next door. He was so busy talking to this (she paused for effect here) PERSON he was with and SHE was dressed so nice. I mean, the dress she was wearing was a bit too tight for my taste, but she had on the cutest red heels I have ever seen."

I felt my eyes widen, and the glimmer in Debbie's eyes told me it delighted her a bit as she said, "Now, I'm sure they were just going in there for some kind of meeting….but those shoes she was wearing… Oh, sorry!"

I didn't know what to say. My mind was racing even faster now wondering who Dan could be with. I had to admit since our relationship had been on the rocks I wondered if somebody else would creep into the picture. Now it seemed my worst fears were coming true. I had run my husband away.

Debbie looked at me and with a wink said, "Well, now, I'm sure it's just completely innocent. Oh, I'm sorry! You were about to leave and I'm keeping you from it. I'll let you enjoy the rest of your day. Bye, honey!" And with that, she WALKED on air back across the street with her six inch high heels clacking off into the distance.

I managed to mumble a "Uh-huh" in reply all the while thinking "What should I do?" I just stood there for a moment, not knowing what to say. I regrouped and got ahold of myself and got in the car. I was going to the grocery store anyway. I wasn't going to change my plans now.

When I got there, sure enough, there was Dan's car still parked in front of the restaurant. Should I get out and go in the restaurant? Surely there was nothing to this. Then again, it was a Chinese restaurant. Now, I knew for a fact that Dan hated Chinese food. What was he doing in there? I was debating with myself about what to do when I saw Dan come walking out with this woman... just the two of them. My heart sank.

I wasn't parked near them but they were going to have to walk right in front of my car! Should I get out? I froze. It was as if everything was happening in slow motion. Dan was so busy talking to her that he never even noticed my car. Unfortunately, I did get a very good look at the woman. And Debbie wasn't lying, she was incredibly attractive in every physical way a woman could be.

This woman was in her twenties, blonde, skinny, and so pretty. She wasn't just pretty, she was stunning. And her body, well... she either had a built-in air pump or they were paid for. Her body was amazing. She was amazing. They got in Dan's car and drove off... together. And I sat in my car feeling more alone than I ever had in my life. It was a mixture of emotions: loneliness, betrayal, anger, sadness and confusion.

I was thinking, "Who can blame him? She's beautiful and I'm..." I had gone to the trouble of fixing my hair and even putting on a little makeup. I was getting dressed to my lace-up shoes. The house was better than it had ever been. I WAS GETTING BETTER! And this is what I get. I suddenly felt worse than I had ever felt in my life. I was crushed. I was working so hard to change and now THIS.

I could feel my makeup smearing as tears ran down my face. I couldn't go in the grocery store now. I was a mess. Desperate, I got my cell phone and called Susan and tried to talk, but she had trouble understanding me through my crying. After about a minute, I managed to coherently blurt out, "I think Dan is having an affair!"

Susan, ever the voice of reason, calmly replied, "Ok, Gina. Just breathe. What are you talking about? What has happened?"

I breathed deeply in and out for a moment then unloaded the entire story to her. She reasoned with me, "Now, Gina. You don't know that situation. There might be a completely logical explanation. Let's not jump to conclusions."

I was still trying to catch my breath.

After about 30 seconds of silence, Susan asked, "Are you still in the parking lot at the grocery store?"

"Yes."

"Stay there. I'm on my way."

"You don't have to come over here. I'm fine. Really, I'm fine." I said through sobs.

Susan insisted, "I'm coming. I'll be right there!"

We hung up. I was still reeling from what I had seen. How would I address this with Dan? Should I call him? Should I march right into his office? Should I say anything at all? I didn't know what to do.

I was so mad at Dan and at myself and to top it off, I felt utterly ugly... worse than I had ever felt in my life. I saw the Burger Barn next door and went through the drive through for a double *cheeseburger, cheesy bacon fries, and a large chocolate Oreo pie with (of course) a Diet Coke. After the day I was having, I was entitled! I had just finished stuffing my face when Susan arrived.*

She got in my car and saw the Burger Barn bags, but she never mentioned them. She hugged me. I sat there and cried for a few minutes.

"Listen to me. It's going to be ok. You've got to hear me. It's going to be ok."

I was trying to believe her. All the things I had just learned last month were bouncing around my brain. All the positive things I had been telling myself seemed meaningless. I felt as low as I had ever felt.

Susan encouraged me again not to jump to conclusions and that perhaps there was a simple explanation for this. I told her how fat and ugly I felt. I told her that she should've seen this girl. She was stunning. How could I compete with her?

Susan reminded me that Dan loved me with all his heart.

I continued my crying, "Oh, Susan! Is it because I've gained this weight when I had the kids?"

Susan interrupted, "Gina! Please listen to me. You need to calm down. I understand you're upset, but listen: I've been exactly where you are. My marriage almost didn't make it. I felt just like you. I thought my husband was losing interest in me and, truthfully, he was. My weight was bad, my clothes were horrible, and my attitude was even worse."

"YOU were overweight??" I blurted.

She smiled back, "Yes. I was." My face was in utter shock. "I lost my weight by changing my eating habits and doing 'loving movements.' I finally realized that taking care of myself was important and gradually my attitude got better. If I wanted to be around to enjoy my children and grandchildren, not to mention have a good life with my husband, I had to learn to take care of myself. I was the only person in the world who could do it. A doctor wasn't going to do it for me. Neither would my children or my mother... or even my husband. I had to want it for myself. I had to realize that I was worth it."

Frustrated, I answered, "But how? I've tried diets before. I've never been able to follow through. I just don't know if I can..."

Susan gently interrupted, "Let's not worry about that right now. You have got to calm down." After sitting there for an hour and talking I was calm enough to drive home. God bless, Susan. She was there when I needed her. I will never forget it.

Dan got home from work that night. Talk about awkward. He acted normal, although his "normal" toward me wasn't all that good. I wanted to ask him about it. I actually started to ask him twice, but I froze. I was afraid of the conflict in front of the kids. So I avoided it. I came upstairs and wrote all this out. Somehow it helped release the pressure of me blowing up at him.

And now, I'm probably going to cry myself to sleep. Not that Dan will ever notice...

Oh, my. How awful. I felt awful for her. This whole thing made me resolve to work harder on my routines, but even harder on my marriage.

My husband and I have had an OK marriage, but if I was honest with myself each year the weight had been inching up. I always

130

thought it was my business, but I guess if I was going to really love myself and my husband then I would have to take better care of myself.

The FlyLady habit for this month was making up my bed. I had actually already been doing that consistently. It felt good to be "caught up" for this month. I focused on my kids making up their own beds every day. We worked together for a while and then they began to take the initiative. I had to remind them a few times but by the end of the month they were doing it all by themselves. Well, most of the time. Kids do what you INspect, not what you EXpect. So, I had to remind myself to inspect and praise often.

It's amazing the difference a made up bed can make in the appearance of a bedroom and it really doesn't take much effort.

I thought about Gina so much. I wondered how she was doing. My schedule didn't allow me to read the diary, but finally I had an afternoon all to myself, so I picked up the diary and sat down and read. It seemed like she was becoming a part of my life.

Chapter 15
Moving in May

Dear Diary,

I didn't sleep very well last night. I was up thinking about all the things I had to work on in my life, particularly my marriage and my health. The clock was glowing with a bright "4:44 AM." I quietly went downstairs and turned on the TV. The only thing on was infomercials about weight loss products and real estate investing. I wasn't going to buy anything. I went back upstairs to try to sleep. I slipped back under the covers, but my mind was still working on everything I needed to be doing.

I lay there, dozing in and out of sleep. I looked at the clock again: 6:15. Susan told me she was usually up by 6:00 every morning. I reached over for my cell phone that was on the charger and sent Susan a text:

"Were you serious about wanting to help me get healthy? I need something to help keep me moving forward."

I looked at the text message and then looked at Dan lying next to me. All I could think about was that home wrecker he was walking with: Thin, beautiful. If I was going to embrace the change I had been learning about, it was time to step up and actually DO something. I had done all the talking a person could do. I had seen firsthand where talking had gotten me and that was nowhere healthy or happy. I decided to make the change. I hit "send."

In about 10 seconds, I had a reply: "Yes."

I replied back, "When?"

In another 10 seconds, Susan replied, "Meet me at the gym on Main Street at 8:45. Wear some workout clothes. Anything will do."

I had no idea what I was in for. I knew I wasn't capable of doing much. My phone buzzed again with another text message:

"Don't worry. We'll take it slow. It's just like everything else: BABY STEPS!" I felt better already.

Dan got up and left for work in his usual manner. I could barely look at him. I was hurting. I wondered if he was going to be with that woman. My mind raced with all sorts of "what if" scenarios, but I was reminded of how Susan told me not to let my mind wander to places it shouldn't. I was going to focus on what was at hand: Taking care of and blessing <u>myself</u> for a change.

I met Susan at the gym. I showed up in sweats and an old T-shirt. Susan was all decked out in cute workout clothes. She looked amazing. I was so proud of her for all she had accomplished. I know a lot of people would be jealous of her, but now I knew where she had come from, and how she had done it one baby step at a time. I knew I could do it too and when I lost my faith in myself, even for a moment, a testimonial or a musing or even one of my little sticky notes reminded me that I was capable. GO ME! She had to get me checked in, but she said she would take care of everything and told me to wait for her by the treadmills.

This was a large gym and they had about 12 of these treadmills in a row. I walked toward the treadmills feeling like there were hundreds of eyes staring at me. Like people were thinking, "Who's the new chubby girl? Why is she here? It isn't New Years, so this can't be a resolution." But as I glanced around, everyone was into their own thing and nobody seemed to notice me at all, which was exactly the way I wanted it.

There were five empty treadmills in a row so I jumped on one in the middle, I didn't want to be close to anybody. I looked at the control panel, which closely resembled an airplane cockpit. I had to make sure I didn't touch the wrong one because I didn't want to go flying into the back wall at 100 MPH and end up on YouTube.

There was a big button in the middle that said "Quick Start." I pressed that and it started the motion. It was very slow, which was fine by me. One button said "speed" and the other said "incline." Neither one sounded appealing so I just left them alone, waiting for Susan to get there.

"Hi! I haven't seen you here before," came a voice from my right.

Some man had gotten on the treadmill right next to me. He was wearing a muscle shirt. Before you get excited, he must've been 70. His arms were huge and covered with white hair. The hair growing out of the front of his shirt made it look like he had stuffed a small Yorkie dog down the front of it and he was scrambling to get out. In other words, "YUCK!" Ok… so who was I to judge anyone?

I didn't really know what to say. Thankfully, Susan was right there. "Ok, Charlie, leave her alone. She's with me and she's married. Go on now. You heard me, scoot!"

I was shocked at her straightforwardness, but thankful for her intervention in an awkward moment. The old guy chuckled and walked off. It was obviously not his first time being scolded by a woman. Susan confirmed this, "He's a regular here. Ignore him."

She looked at my treadmill and bumped the speed to "2" and said, "Don't worry. We're starting slow."

135

Then she carried on a conversation with me about the kids, school, and my life. She complimented me on my house and my progress. We talked a little while (and very discreetly) about Dan. She told me again to take things a day at a time. We talked about me going back to teaching and the plans I was making to get back into it.

I was talking about how much weight I was wanting to lose when all of the sudden Susan reached over and hit the "Stop" button on my treadmill and announced, "Ok, you're done."

"Done? You mean done for the day??"

"Yes," she replied.

"How can that be it?" I asked. "That was only..." I looked at my timer on the treadmill and it was at 15:02. Fifteen minutes and two seconds.

Susan instructed, "It's just like your cleaning. You can do <u>anything</u> *for 15 minutes. Besides, you just did one mile!" The counter clearly said otherwise. I started to ask, but knowing Susan, she would explain it.*

We left the gym together and on the way to the car I asked Susan, "We're going to do this every day for 15 minutes?"

"Oh, no. Not at all. As a matter of fact, you don't ever have to come back here unless you just want to. It's not about working out at a gym every day. The habit for May is called, 'Moving in May.' Here, I have something for you."

She handed me a small device that looked like a digital clock with a hook on it.

Susan explained, "It's a pedometer. It registers the steps you take. FlyLady has a system called 'Moving in May.' It's fun and it's a great way for people who don't normally exercise to start small and move into taking care of themselves. Just like we learned to take care of our home... Baby Steps. For every 15 minutes you walk, it counts toward one mile on FlyLady's virtual journey. The tour starts in North Carolina where FlyLady lives. You go to her website and the information is there. You always end up in some exciting places. It makes the exercise more fun when you know members from around the world are moving with you."

It didn't sound very hard; I agreed to do it. Besides, FlyLady made everything fun. I went back home and did my normal routines. I did my cleaning routines, picked the kids up from school, took them to their practices, went to the grocery store, then went home. When I got home, I realized I had actually forgotten to turn off the pedometer! To my shock, I had walked two miles! I didn't even know it!

I logged in my time with FlyLady on her website. It was really easy to do. When I posted my times, I received a message that gave me hints on where we were going on our "Virtual Journey." The journey started in Brevard, North Carolina (FlyLady's home town) and continued to different places. Every time I logged in my minutes I would get another clue as well as descriptions of fun places along the way.

I found walking helped me to clear my head and focus on my activities for the day. Some days I exercised in the afternoon, but the best time for me was usually in the morning after I took the kids to school. After I got back I would enter my time to read about where we were going next on the FlyLady virtual tour.

The places were fun, but what was more amazing was how I started to enjoy my 15 minutes of walking. I read on FlyLady's site that some people just sit in one place and lift small weights and that counted too. I was really enjoying walking. I started finding the hard part was, like my 15-minute cleaning blitzes, stopping after just 15 minutes. Before I knew it, my 15 minute walks were turning into longer and longer walks. I was enjoying listening to the world around me and breathing in the fresh air. Some days I left my pedometer on and I was amazed at how far I walked just by doing the things I always did. I was losing weight and firming up. I was hoping Dan would notice but he never said a word. I kept reminding myself, "I am doing this for me!" Go ME!

A few days ago, he called at 5:00 PM to tell me he wouldn't be home for supper. Something just didn't feel right. I asked him what he was going to do for supper and he said he was going to eat with a coworker. He said the meeting at work today had left some unresolved issues and they had to continue the discussions over dinner.

"Coworker?" My mind was racing. Could it be that woman? I asked, "Where are you going to eat?"

"Antonio's" he answered with a frustrated tone. I could tell he was getting very irritated with me. Antonio's was an Italian restaurant. An Italian restaurant?? They had one of those violinists there! It was a romantic place! Not that Dan had a romantic bone in his body. There was NO WAY I was going to just sit there and let that home wrecker steal my husband. The time had come to confront both of them.

Brittany was helping me more around the house and that day she was feeding the little ones. I told her I had to run an errand. I was going to show up and catch him in the act. I was NOT living this way. I drove over to Antonio's. Dan's car was outside. I pulled in and parked near his car. I took a deep breath to steel my nerves.

I entered the restaurant and was greeted by the maître d'. I told him I was looking for someone and he told me to help myself. I walked around the wall and there was Dan, with his back to me, talking to a woman. My heart sank.

It didn't look like the same woman that was in the other place, though. As I got closer I could hear their conversation. I realized the woman was actually the restaurant manager. Dan's order was evidently messed up and she was there to apologize.

Dan was seated at a two-person table but there was nobody on the other side from him. I bet that blonde woman was in the bathroom. I was going to find out shortly. I walked up behind Dan and tapped him on the shoulder as I said in a sarcastic tone, "Hello, Dan."

He was shocked to see me there. "Gina?? What are you doing here?"

I was just about to answer the question when Dan's dinner guest walked up to our table. It was Allen. He and Dan had worked together for 19 years.

"Gina! This is a wonderful surprise!" Allen exclaimed, "Are you joining us?"

I was about to answer. I suppose I hadn't even thought about it when I left the house, but I suddenly became aware that I was wearing a T-shirt and sweatpants in the middle of a four star restaurant. I was also painfully aware that everyone was staring at me. I'm sure it was an embarrassment to Dan too. I felt like a complete idiot.

*I finally managed to mutter, "Uh, I just came by because I was going to the grocery store and I... ugh... forgot my... uh.........
purse (I was able to latch on to some excuse) and I need to borrow yours... I mean borrow some money."*

Dan had a bewildered look on his face.

I recognized Dan's irritated look as he got out his wallet and handed me some cash. I also recognized what that look meant for me when he got home. It was not going to be pleasant at our house tonight. I drove back home feeling mortified. I let all my unfounded suspicions drive me to do something that was embarrassing for my husband and humiliating for me, but something inside me just had to know.

That night when Dan got home, he came up to the bedroom, looked at me and said, "What in the world was that at the restaurant? Have you completely lost your mind??"

Was this it? Was I going to confront him about the woman from the other day? I probably should have... but I didn't. I just made another lame excuse, watched Dan roll his eyes at me, and walk away muttering something under his breath.

I talked to Susan the next day about letting my emotions get the best of me. Dan didn't really talk to me for the next three days. It's been two weeks since it happened and although things are a bit strained, we are talking and that's progress.

On a more positive note, it's been a few weeks since I started my daily "living movement" and I am very pleased with my progress! I only wish Dan would notice, but I was reminded of why I was doing this. I wasn't getting in shape for him, I was getting in shape for ME and I wasn't quitting this time. I was learning to

give myself the pats on the back for doing a good job and not
acting like a martyr when Dan didn't notice.

I know I need to exercise. The first thing I did was go on the
FlyLady site and find information on "Moving in May." I didn't
have a pedometer (I wasn't exactly sure I could pick one out in
the store if I saw it on the shelf) but I was determined I was
going to walk for 15 minutes a day. I figured I could do anything
for 15 minutes.

Afternoons were the best time for me to walk. It's odd, but
walking seemed to clear my mind. After doing this for three
weeks, I made a choice that it would become a daily part of my
life, but I wasn't going to be a perfectionist about it. And it really
does NOT take much for the exercise to kick in and make you
feel better. I was beginning to feel different, happier.

Each day that I did my walks I had more energy to get through
the rest of my day. My mind seemed sharper and I generally
enjoyed my day more. By the end of the month I was even
considering adding in some sort of other type of exercise. I said I
was CONSIDERING it. I didn't say I did it, but still... that was
another Baby Step in the right direction.

After an afternoon walk I picked up the diary and started
reading to see what happened to Gina. What I was about to read
proved to be very interesting.

Dear Diary,

After four weeks, my walks have become a part of my life. I really
look forward to them and I can honestly say that I enjoy them
now. I have lost several pounds and I'm very proud of myself.

I was talking with Susan about my weight loss and how I had done my Moving in May. I was impressed with how far my "Virtual Journey" with the FlyLady had taken me. We had visited some interesting places in May.

But Susan told me that just doing movement would not get me to my goal. She said there was a 'missing key' that unlocked the door to the weight loss I wanted. I had to combine two other things to make it there.

"What is the missing key, Susan?" I asked.

Chapter 16
The Missing Key

"The missing key is...eating right. And you have to do two specific things. You have to eat healthy. As close to natural as possible."

Immediately my mind jumped to all the diets and fads I had tried. None of them worked for me. Besides, how could you possibly know what the "right thing to eat" really was?

Susan told me this could be a confusing thing to study, but based on her experience and weight loss she would tell me what worked for her.

"Gina, this is going to involve some lifestyle changes. I had to give up certain things I liked.

"Most of the time when you think you are hungry, you are probably thirsty. Many people are dehydrated and they don't even know it."

I nodded, "What about eating right? How do you really know what's right?"

"For me, after doing some studying, I really felt that eliminating bad carbs was the way to go. I began to eat more protein, like chicken, turkey, and fish. The bad carbs I eliminated were things like white bread, sweets, and pastas, which was my weakness! I also quit drinking sodas. At first, all I did was eliminate sodas and I actually lost several pounds from nothing but that!"

My head sank because I loved my sodas. Susan continued, "Remember, Gina. BABY STEPS! If you're drinking three sodas a day, try cutting back to one or two. Do that for a week. Try limiting your carb intake. Remember: if it comes in a box, it's probably not good for you."

I wanted to know, "Isn't a low carb diet bad for your heart and your cholesterol?"

"There's actually research that says a diet low in bad, unhealthy carbohydrates and high in protein is good for your heart, but I encourage everyone to talk to their doctor and ask them what they feel is best for them. The bottom line is: it worked for me. I lost 40 pounds doing a low carb lifestyle and increasing my water intake to a proper level."

"I can do it. It's just hard for me because I REALLY like my food. Sometimes when I'm down it just makes me feel better."

Susan kindly responded, "We are supposed to eat for nourishment, not comfort." She told me, "This is another way to love yourself. You are loving your body."

I hadn't thought of it in those terms before. It made sense to me. I decided I would do it. I had already done so much and made so many changes, what was one more? Besides, after all I had been through in the last month with Dan, I knew this was an area I truly needed to change.

"I'll try the diet."

"That's great," said Susan with some hesitancy, telling me there was more coming, "but instead of a diet, I'd like for you to think of this as more of a lifestyle change. Diets don't usually work because they have a beginning and an end. And after the end usually comes the rebound." (I knew this all too well! I had been through that pattern so many times!) "When you make a lifestyle change, *you've made some positive decisions for your life that will impact you the rest of your life. I KNOW you can do it, Gina!"*

Susan gave me some great ideas for limiting bad carbs. She even went shopping with me at the grocery store to help me find the right things. I began eating like she suggested. At first it was a bit weird. I did get a headache on a few days. Susan said this was just my body getting rid of toxins and other things that didn't need to be there in the first place.

I downloaded some podcasts to listen to during my afternoon walks. Some were of the FlyLady, others were from Dr. Gary Taubes and the Livin' La Vida Low Carb Show. They were fun to listen to. I also downloaded some of my favorite music. It really got me going in the mornings. Combining my walking and exercise with my new diet had some amazing results on my body.

The first week was not much of a change. On weeks two and three I had dropped several pounds! I was amazed! The best part was when Brittany told me she was proud of me for losing the weight. She also told me my clothes looked "frumpy" and I needed to go shopping for some new ones.

We had a mother/daughter outing the next day and Brittany helped me pick out some outfits that were my size. I almost cried when I walked out of the dressing room and looked in that full-length mirror. I could really see my body changes. Brittany told me to surprise her Dad by wearing one of my new outfits tomorrow. She even helped me fix my hair and makeup. We were bonding in ways I had only previously dreamed of and I loved every minute of it!

The next day I looked in the mirror. It looked like a different person staring back at me. My weight loss had now exceeded my expectations! I was really making progress. I fixed a special dinner that night for the family.

Dan, as usual, walked in the door on his cell phone talking to a client. He walked right past me and never looked at me. My heart sank. Brittany could see the disappointment and said, "He's just focused on the phone, Mom. You know how he is when he's on his phone."

Very true. He had a one-track mind that could only focus on one thing at a time. I tried not to let my heart sink. I had Karly and Ethan and Brittany sit down at the table. Dan finally came in, sat down and started talking to Ethan.

I asked him what he wanted to drink. He replied, "Iced Tea," finally looking up at me.

He did a double take. I mean an actual DOUBLE take. He looked at me as if it was the first time he had ever seen me. I got chills. Brittany saw it too and smiled and winked at me.

I went right on putting food on the table as though I hadn't even noticed his reaction. We ate and had some great conversation. Dan continued looking at me during the meal. He would look away when I would look at him as if he didn't want me to know he was noticing me. I have to confess, I was enjoying his attention.

I got up to put the dishes in the dishwasher after dinner. Dan was standing behind me and asked, "Have you lost weight?"

"Some," I replied unassertively.

"Well, you look really good. Keep it up."

And with that, he walked into the living room. I was facing the sink, holding back tears. It probably was a backhanded compliment, but my husband thought I looked good... just not good enough yet. I couldn't remember the last time he had complimented me like that. No matter what, though, I reminded myself that I was doing it for me, not him or anybody else. I was taking care of ME.

Over the next week Dan would make comments on my appearance. Every time it made me feel good. We were talking a lot more these days. I was keeping up my new lifestyle of exercising and having an eating plan. One of the things I quickly discovered is that if I don't have a meal plan then I'm apt to eat poorly. Spontaneous eating is normally BAD eating.

FlyLady had some great resources on meal plans by Leanne Ely, so I just used hers. They were very easy to do and I was able to apply my choices to her meal plans and add them to my Control Journal. Having a plan helped me stick with everything. I had a momentum with my health that I hadn't had before.

Dan went from talking to me to actually flirting. It was like we were dating again. He even asked me to be his "date" for a company party! It felt so wonderful!

I had a week and a half to prepare for the party. I bought a new dress. Brittany helped me pick it out. It was a "little black dress." I had always wanted to wear a little black dress, but never could. This dress was three sizes smaller than I normally wore. It felt so good to shop for smaller sizes! Finally, the night arrived for the big date. We drove over to the hotel where they were having the party in the grand ballroom. After we parked the car, Dan held my hand on the way into the hotel!

The room was beautifully decorated. There were trees with miniature white lights in them surrounding the room. In the middle of the room was a dance floor surrounded on two sides by a jazz band playing soft music. On the other side was a beautifully decorated buffet table capped with intricately carved ice sculptures on both ends. There were soft blue lights shining on the walls, and flowers and candles on every table in the room. It had such a romantic glow. We walked around, hand in hand, talking to people. Every now and then Dan would let go of my hand and hold me around my waist. It's as if, for the first time in a long time, he was proud to have me there. He was even introducing me to his coworkers as "his wife" which is something he hadn't done in a long time.

And then I saw HER from across the room. Yes, HER. THAT home wrecker! The woman I had seen Dan with at the Chinese restaurant. I watched her spot Dan and come running over. I started getting a sick feeling in the pit of my stomach. Was she about to ruin my otherwise perfect night?

She came up to Dan and me and said, "Hi, Mr. Thomas!" Dan introduced me to her, "Gina, this is Buffy." "Buffy?" That didn't sound like a name. It sounded like a household cleaning product.

Before I could reply, Buffy bubbled over as she said, "Oh, Mrs. Thomas! It's SO nice to finally meet you. Mr. Thomas has been so wonderful to help me. I was doing an internship here. I'm about to move to Chicago in a few weeks. I see what he's been talking about with you. He told me how pretty you were! He's been so good to me and my..." She stopped and looked over her shoulder and called out, "Darren!" and motioned for a tall, handsome young man in his early twenties to join us. Dan introduced me, "Gina, this is Buffy's fiancé, Mr. Wonderful... I mean, Darren." Buffy giggled with delight.

I extended my hand to Darren and Buffy and said, "It's so nice to meet you."

Buffy chimed in, "Darren just finished school and has been hired to manage a large department in a company in Chicago. We're getting married in a few weeks and then we're going to start our lives there. I'm so proud of him! And Mr. Thomas recommended me for a job at a sister company in Chicago!"

"That's so sweet of you to help them," I commented, looking at Dan with a glowing admiration and love and with the realization of knowing he wasn't having an affair after all. I was so relieved.

"Yeah," she continued, "Darren's been working hard managing this Chinese restaurant next door to the big grocery store on Conway Avenue. I try to eat there every day just to see him." And holding up her ring finger triumphantly to show off a very small but sparkling diamond ring she repeated herself, "And... we're getting married!" She was positively giddy.

"Oh, boy," I thought. THAT's why they were at the restaurant that day! Dan spoke up, "We're very proud of you, Buffy, and we wish you and Darren all the best. I know you'll do extremely well."

Buffy and Darren thanked Dan and then went off to enjoy the party. I had totally misconstrued the entire event. It made me think about the other times in my life I had jumped to the wrong conclusion and "flown off the handle." I would make a concerted effort from this point on to act calmly and not react to situations before I had all the details.

That night the room glowed, the band played, and Dan and I danced to a beautiful rendition of "Moonlight Serenade." It was magical. I felt like a teenager all over again. Later that night as we *entered the house, he looked deeply into my eyes, told me I was beautiful, and then kissed me. For obvious reasons, I won't describe the rest of my night, but let's just say it was the most romantic, amazing night I've had in years.*

I was so happy for Gina. How wonderful for her! I looked up some information on Gary Taubes and I found the Livin' La Vida Low Carb Show hosted by Jimmy Moore. I found out the difference between good carbs and bad carbs. I had no idea. The habit from FlyLady for this month was drinking your water. I committed myself to do this and put some reminders on my phone to help me remember.

This healthy eating thing really worked! I had lost weight and was feeling good. I had also lost two dress sizes! I didn't do the shopping spree that Gina did, but Bobby took me out to buy a new dress. It was hard to choose which one because I must have tried on 25 of them and he liked them all. He's such a sweetheart. He lit up every time I walked out of the dressing room. His reactions made me feel more like a Victoria's Secret runway model than a middle-aged mom.

I couldn't wait to read what happened to Gina next. I just knew great things were ahead for her. What I didn't realize was that great things were ahead for me too!

Chapter 17
The Last Great Battle!

Dear Diary,

I'm still reeling from my "magical" night with Dan. It's like we're 16 again. I love him more today than I ever have. He kissed me goodbye this morning on his way to work and told me he'd see me tonight. I'm going to change my menu plans and fix him his favorite dinner.

I got up this morning and began my routines. It's nice to have most of the clutter out of my way. I read in my FlyLady email that the habit for this month was "Swish and Swipe" the bathroom. Instead of detail cleaning everything, you go through and swipe the counters and swish the toilets with a toilet brush.

I went through the bathrooms each day swiping off the sinks, countertops, and swishing the toilets. It was really no trouble at all to add this small thing to my daily routines. Who would have thought such a small thing would keep the bathrooms so clean?

I have to say as I look around my home, it really looks better. I would even go so far as to call it "clean." It makes me feel nervous to say it, as if the ceiling is going to fall in and suddenly things will start piling up again, but I know the key is just what FlyLady said, "Do my daily routines and put things up when I'm finished with them." I know one thing for sure: I like being caught up much better than constantly running to catch up. If I get haphazard and rushed and forget to put things away, I just do a 15 minute room rescue. I rush through the house and put things away that I find sitting left out.

I'm off to the grocery store to get what I need for Dan's special meal tonight. But before I leave, I have to say, I'm happy with my home and the progress I've made.

I'll write more later.

"Swish and Swipe the bathroom huh?" For me it's a bit more like "Bulldoze and dump the whole house!" I do understand the principle though and I've made a lot of progress. It definitely isn't perfect, but from everything I've been learning "perfect" is a word I need to let go of. If I try to do it perfectly, deep inside I know I can't accomplish that and I will fail, so I procrastinate the work to save myself the trauma of failing again. I'm learning to catch myself in my perfectionism moments. I'm using a mantra over and over in my head that FlyLady says: I love myself and good enough is "Good Enough". I know now that I deserve a clean, joyful home.

I've been continuing to declutter my zones. It's not so much the stuff; it's the clothes. I have clothes everywhere. It seems like as soon as I clean one set of clothes another one rises up in its place. I've never been able to handle laundry. It's just a never-ending mound of dirty clothes that multiplies itself every single day.

I'll even confess that several times I've actually gone out and bought other clothes because I didn't have any clean ones available. I figured we would need them eventually. Ok, it was really much easier to buy new clothes than to wash all the mounds of laundry on my floor because it took so long to get it all done.

Then there have been the countless times I've started a load in the washer and have left them there too long because I got distracted. They mildewed and stunk worse than they did before I washed them! I had to wash them all over again. I seemed to have a real problem with this. Bobby would always complain about the smell if I left them in the washer for too long.

What can you do with clothes? It's not like the other stuff I've decluttered. It seemed wasteful to throw away the clothes, especially after the small fortune I had invested in them. I noticed the FlyLady habit for the next month was "Laundry." It looked like it was going to come in the nick of time. I picked up the diary and looked ahead a few pages. It was a bit surprising.

Dear Diary,

The FlyLady habit for this month is laundry. I used to have a real problem here. It's still painful to think back to how things used to be. Mounds of laundry all over the house. Piles of dirty clothes, piles of clean clothes that hadn't been folded and put away, a load of dried clothes still in the dryer, and a load of mildewed clothes that had been in the washer about three days too long. I was living in "Mount Washmore" as FlyLady calls it. You know she really makes me laugh with all her fun little sayings. Here's one: "When it's fun, the work gets done!" Who ever thought housework would be fun?

I used to feel laundry was a never-ending job that was impossible to complete. Then I learned a simple secret that helped me get caught up.

That's exactly how I feel! I was laughing about "Mount Washmore." I was actually looking at the monument in my house on my dining room table. If I looked closely I could see my four kids' faces in the mountain. But what was the simple secret?? I read on:

I remember when I was struggling in a sea of laundry. I hadn't noticed it as much because it was just so much a part of my life

153

that I simply accepted. Susan called me to talk about something and in the process of the conversation she asked what I was doing and I replied, "Laundry Day."

"How long does it take you to do all your laundry?" she asked.

"Easily eight hours."

"EIGHT HOURS?"

I wondered why that was a surprise to her, with the size of my family.

"It sounds like you do all your laundry on one day!"

"Most of the time, I do. I may wash a few things like baseball uniforms or other outfits the kids need, but I mostly do my laundry on Saturday. When do you do yours, Susan?"

"Every day."

"What???"

"Seriously. Every day. I got it from FlyLady. I do one load a day, every day. It keeps things from piling up and helps me stay ahead."

"How in the world do you find time to fold all that stuff every day?"

"I don't do a huge load every day. At first it was hard to catch up. But this is just like everything else. It's much easier to maintain than it is to catch up. And to answer your question, I fold very little. One of the tips I got from FlyLady was that it takes much less time to put something on the hanger than it does to fold it."

"You must have some major closet space to hang up all that stuff!"

"I actually got rid of some clothes. Once I started looking through my closet I realized there were a lot of things I didn't even wear or need. I donated them to charity. It blessed them and blessed my house. I had plenty of room in my closet once I decluttered."

"How many outfits do you have?"

"I personally have 10."

I started thinking "10?" I knew for a fact I had over 30 in my closet.

Susan continued, "Think about it, Gina. You don't really need more than 10 outfits. You can't wear more than one at a time! And 10 nice outfits will give you enough to wear Monday through Friday for two full weeks."

I did exactly what she said. It took a little more than two weeks for me to get a handle on my laundry but it's been much easier since then.

Time for me to put this down and get back to my studies. I have a big test coming up tomorrow for my teaching degree. I'm getting closer to my dream!

Declutter my clothes? I decided to set aside a day to go through my closet. I started the day by pulling out clothes I couldn't wear anymore. I had some clothes I was holding onto for "inspiration" to get some of my weight off but after looking at my "thin" clothes I realized I wouldn't wear the majority of them anyway. They were out of style. I threw them in a pile.

155

I thought about what Gina had written and decided to pull out ten outfits that I really liked. I wasn't looking forward to this. I liked my clothes. I didn't know how I was going to part with all the ones I loved. This turned out to be a very sobering moment for me.

I went through my closet looking for my ten outfits and I only had six that I actually wore. The rest had some reason attached to it for why I didn't wear it; too tight, scratchy, too short, wrong color... you know what I mean. They were sitting in my closet doing NO good. I couldn't believe it! I felt ashamed and very selfish. I was hoarding clothes as well as other stuff I didn't need. I put together some outfits I loved and began to sort out the rest of them.

Then I began to wonder how many of my kids had clothes they didn't need either. I had the kids go through their closet and pick out their ten favorite outfits. I helped my youngest pick out her ten. The two middle ones came up with seven outfits each, and my teenager came up with three (naturally). After going back in her room with her, we managed to up that to six.

I had them put their unneeded outfits in large garbage bags to take them to two local shelters: one for battered women and one for the homeless. My baby had the hardest time with giving things away but once I explained to her that we were helping those less fortunate people, she got a smile on her face and offered to help pack everything up. I even had to go back and check her closet to make sure she didn't give EVERYTHING she owned away. I love her precious little heart.

Once we decluttered our clothes, it made it much easier to get a handle on the laundry because there is plenty of room to put things away now. I started doing one load a day. After a couple of weeks I had conquered "Mount Washmore." I think I knew how a general felt after winning a decisive victory. I surveyed the clean room that was formally occupied by the enemy forces of socks, underwear, shirts, and pants. And now I am pleased to report that the enemy forces have been eradicated.

I have reclaimed "Mount Washmore!" The dining room table, previously full of stacks of clothes, was now mine again! I have won a great battle for my home. It's a good feeling! Go me!!

Chapter 18
Freedom

Dear Diary,

The FlyLady habit for this month is the before bedtime routine. I made mine several months ago and it has been so valuable in helping me feel like I'm ready for the next day. I've kept using my FlyLady calendar and Control Journal and it has kept me on track. Things are easier when you're able to see your days, weeks, and months laid out for you. It also helps me avoid the embarrassment of missing important events for my family and myself.

My before bedtime routine was the key in me losing weight, being on time with the kids, and keeping my day organized. It's evolved as the year has gone on so I'll spend a day this month updating and revising it, but it has been so good for me. During the first month I was keeping up with my routines by using sticky notes posted all over the house. Not effective, but functional. Once I got my calendar I wrote them on there, but that was a lot of trouble to write every day. Now my routines are written in my Control Journal where I can see them.

I've been teaching now for the last two months. Between Dan, the kids, and teaching, I haven't had much time to write anymore. Things are going so well at the teaching job. It's my dream come true. The students seemed to be as nervous as I was the first day, but we've gotten to know each other and their parents are very sweet. I truly love what I'm doing.

I volunteer at the hospital occasionally when my schedule allows. I visit children and parents in the children's ward as well as the elderly patients. It feels so good to be able to give my time doing worthwhile things instead of fretting over my house and other things. FlyLady was right: it's SO much easier to maintain than it is to live in CHAOS.

For many years, I felt as if my house was my prison with no doors and no windows. Through taking those Baby Steps I am free, free to FLY and be the "me" I was meant to be.

I always believed freedom from clutter and CHAOS was something that was meant for superwomen, like Susan and FlyLady and other people I read about. I didn't think I was capable, much less deserving of this type of freedom.

Part of being a good teacher is being a good student. FlyLady has been a wonderful mentor. She gave me something money absolutely couldn't buy: knowledge, truth, and peace. Now it is my privilege to pass along knowledge and truth to those I come in contact with. I think it is one of the highest forms of love there is. Sometimes the hardest thing to do is believe in yourself enough to step out and help someone else.

That sounded good to me. "Peace…Freedom." It's something I've always wanted. Unlike Gina, though, I wasn't sure what freedom would look like for me. I definitely wasn't cut out to be a teacher. They say everybody has a dream, I just don't know what mine is. I would have to think on that one for a while. I can't even remember when I have allowed myself to dream about my own wants and wishes.

My husband wanted to have a party at the house. Nine months ago I would have absolutely FREAKED OUT at that thought. But now, my house was looking decent. Again, not perfect (not that there's any such thing as that), but good enough to have company. Bobby had commented numerous times about how good the house looked. I couldn't tell if he was just being nice. But you know, I think the peace is beginning to affect him too.

I spent some time planning the party. I still had some clutter I needed to get rid of before I could host it. I had an old grandfather clock that hadn't worked in two years. I couldn't let that just sit there. I had Bobby help me take it to the garage. As I walked into the garage my jaw dropped.

It was full of stuff. I hadn't walked through there in a while. I guess I had become immune to the mess. I usually just walked out the front door to get to the car. I had forgotten all about the garage. This thing was packed full of clutter!

There was years of stuff stacked up in that garage. There was no way I could let anybody in there. I would close the garage door and block the exit from the house with some decorations. It would work. It <u>had</u> to work!

The night of the party arrived. My house looked great (if I do say so myself!) and the guests were having a great time. Everything was going smoothly until my youngest daughter decided to come entertain our guests. Don't get me wrong, she is funny. But then she proceeded to show our guests her doll collection, which happened to be (you guessed it!) in our garage.

She was already there before I realized where she was going. I tried to stop her without making too big of a scene, but it was too late. I saw two guests (both women) whose horrified face told me and everybody else how cluttered and messy my garage was. I, of course, was mortified. There really wasn't even a path from our door out of the garage. Everybody smiled politely but I was completely ashamed. I apologized to Bobby. He reassured me saying, "Honey, lots of people have messy garages."

It didn't help. I was truly embarrassed, but I determined I wouldn't let it happen again. I thought my laundry was my last great battle, but it was actually my garage. I was going to make a plan and get it done.

I thought about the freedom Gina talked about. I wanted that. That meant I couldn't get comfortable with where I was. I had to press through and finish this. I was going to conquer that garage and have a totally clean house. No hiding places, no secret stashes of clutter nagging at me saying, "You will never be good enough!" I wanted freedom... from all of it.

I sat down and wrote out everything I needed to do to be ready for the next day. I only wrote out my day to day, every morning stuff. I also left a few blanks for extra stuff that popped up unexpectedly. I knew if I was going to achieve freedom that this was part of it.

The organizational part that seemed to come slowly to Gina was coming easier for me. I actually liked making a list and checking off the items as I finished them. I enjoyed it. I remember alphabetizing books when I was a kid and even making to-do lists. When the kids came along, I got overwhelmed and lost my way. I wondered if my love of organizing could be a clue to finding out what I was really meant to do?

Those thoughts would have to wait until tomorrow. I was going to dive into my garage and get it done. I made a list for decluttering my garage. I actually made a plan of attack. I didn't leave out my regular Before Bedtime Routine either. I laid out all the stuff I needed for my day to start smoothly for my family. It eliminated us being late as well as stopped most of the morning arguments with the kids and me.

The morning came and I read my checklist, going through everything one step at a time. There was a certain peace of mind I had from doing this checklist. I wasn't worried about forgetting things like I had been. I got the kids up and they got themselves ready for school with the clothes we had laid out last night. I had breakfast things all set aside so that part was much easier. I put the dishes directly into the dishwasher and was thankful for my clean counter and sink. They made me smile.

The kids' book bags were at the front door. Getting them to school went off without a hitch (other than my daughter not liking her shoes and begging me to buy her new ones). I was back home very quickly and opened the door to my garage and looked at what loomed before me: a cluttered mess. But I was determined I was going to conquer it. I had my list. I was ready.

It was time for my morning 15 minute break, so rather than jumping in with both feet, I set my timer, made a cup of tea and read the last entry in the Diary.

Chapter 19
Law vs. Grace

Dear Diary,

It's hard to believe it's been a year since we became such great friends. I have enjoyed our conversations. You've helped me get my thoughts out of my head and to a place where they make sense and I actually do something about them. I want to thank you for our times together. You have given me clarity and accountability.

As I've gone back today and reread the last year of my life, I've been astounded at the progress. I truly am not the person I was when I started this journey. Wherever you are FlyLady, I thank you for saving me from my world of CHAOS and giving me a life I wasn't even capable of dreaming of.

I was going to file this diary and keep it in a secret place for me to look at from time to time, but my teacher's heart told me not to do that. After all FlyLady poured into me, I felt like I needed to share this knowledge with someone else. Maybe this diary could be an encouragement and a "mentor" to someone.

That's when I decided to give it away. I prayed it would help someone else out of their pain and embarrassment. Hopefully it has helped you in some small way. Every journey belongs to each individual, but if some of my steps can help make yours easier, then it has been worth it. I originally thought I was writing this all down for me. Now, I know God meant it for you.

I only ask one thing: If this has helped you, pass it and my mentor's book (The FlyLady Sink Reflections book I told you about) along to somebody else. I hope you find joy in all you do. I'm off to teach my class and afterwards visit some brave people that I've come to love and appreciate. I'm living my dream and I wish the same thing for you.

Keep Baby Stepping and moving forward. Know that as you read this, you are not alone, and that you are capable and loved.

Gina

I closed the diary and was thankful these books had come into my hands. The FlyLady book was wonderful and the diary helped me understand that I could do it too. I was changing into a different person. I have the FlyLady, her website, her book, and this diary as my mentor.

Now that I've completed all the monthly habits, I decided to review them:

January:	Shining Your Sink
February:	Declutter for 15 Minutes
March:	Getting Dressed to Lace Up Shoes
April:	Making Your Bed
May:	Moving In May
June:	Drinking Your Water
July:	Swish and Swipe
August:	Laundry
September:	Before Bed Routine
October:	Paper Clutter
November:	Menu Planning
December:	Pampering

The 31 Baby Steps have become pretty automatic for me. I've made progress. There was one more thing I saw in the FlyLady book though. It was called "FlyLady's Eleven Commandments." I was familiar with the "Ten Commandments" but I hadn't heard FlyLady's, and they are pretty key in making life a breeze.

1. Keep your sink clean and shiny.
2. Get dressed every morning, even if you don't feel like it. Don't forget your lace up shoes!
3. Do your morning and before bedtime routine every day.
4. Don't allow yourself to be sidetracked by the computer.
5. Pick up after yourself. If you get it out, put it away.
6. Don't try two projects at once. ONE JOB AT A TIME!
7. Don't pull out more than you can put back in one hour.
8. Do something for yourself every day, maybe even morning and night.
9. Work as fast as you can to get the job done. This will give you more time to play later.
10. Smile even when you don't feel like it. It's contagious! Make up your mind to be happy and you will be!
11. Don't forget to laugh every day. Pamper yourself. You deserve it!

I needed to do better on a few of them. While I was mostly successful in doing the Baby Steps and the Monthly Habit, I needed work in these other areas. I was bad about doing more than one project at a time. I didn't think about laughing and smiling every day. That could really help me! And I was VERY bad about getting sidetracked by the computer. (I like games!)

I was thinking of how to add these commandments into my life, but one of the great things about the whole FlyLady system is that it truly isn't a system of laws. My definition of a law is "a rule you're supposed to keep and you're punished if you don't keep it." I already had enough guilt working in my day-to-day life. I didn't need any more.

But every time I didn't complete a Baby Step or my routines, I was reminded by her emails that always said the same thing at the end, "You are not behind! I don't want you to try and catch up; I just want you to jump in where we are. OK?"

This one thing gave me permission to not feel bad when I "broke a law." I was able to forgive myself, pick it back up where I was, and just keep moving. My personality is normally if I make one mistake then I just quit because I feel I can't do it right. Like every time I was committed to doing a diet: I skipped one meal and felt so bad about it that night that I ate half a box of ice cream and never looked back.

It's safe to say I have perfectionistic tendencies. If I can't be "perfect" then I normally don't attempt it. But FlyLady's system gave me permission NOT to be perfect. Perfection is an illusion. It's just like the magician I saw one time when he levitated a lady. To my eyes it looked so real but I knew there were smoke, mirrors, and wires somewhere.

That's how perfection has been for me. It's been this "THING" I've sought after and was never able to grab hold of. I've been saying my house looks "good but not perfect." I've decided that is good enough for me. I've let go of perfection. I've released it. I can work on me. I can grow as a person, but perfection is no longer something I'm seeking. I'm just determining every single day of my life to give my best on what I'm doing and not worry about the rest. It's very freeing to let go of it. Yes, I still catch myself nearly every day slipping into perfectionism but... I'm getting better and better.

Now on to my garage: I dove in with my list in hand. I opened the door and began to write down what I needed to get rid of and what I needed to keep. Then I did it. I borrowed a truck. Bobby came home and helped me load the stuff into the truck. I was loading things up when Bobby asked, "Where are you taking all this?"

"To the city dump, I guess."

Bobby replied, while pointing to an old table I didn't really like anymore, "I can see that with some of this junk, but that table you have there might be worth something to someone."

I couldn't imagine who would want it, but maybe he was right.

"You're always going to those antique stores. Do you think any of them would be interested in this? I think they might." Bobby persuaded.

Then it hit me: The man at the junk store that sold me the trunk! I could take this stuff to him! He might like it and want to sell it. He was very nice and helpful to me. What was his name? Frank? No. Fred. I would take it to Fred. I drove the truck to the old junk store. It hadn't changed a bit.

I walked into the store and the familiar musty smell reminded me of my visit all those months ago. The bell attached to the door chimed out as the door shut behind me. I heard the old man's voice bellow from the middle of the large room, "Come on in! I'm over here!"

I was anticipating seeing him again and telling him about my things for sale. I came around the corner of an end display of porcelain figurines in a glass case to see the kind old man sitting on a stool. It was great seeing him again and he immediately greeted me with, "Well if it ain't my favorite greenhorn? How are you doing?" I was shocked that he actually remembered me.

He didn't look quite the same. He seemed a little weaker than I remembered. I dismissed it as not feeling well. His eyes danced with the same enthusiasm as before. I greeted him with a big "Hello, Fred! It's good to see you again!"

"What can I do for you today, little lady?"

"I have some things in the truck I'm thinking of selling and I wanted to see if they might be worth anything to you."

"Well, that's what I'm here for! Let's go look," Fred replied. And with that he stood up from his stool and reached behind the counter for a cane and limped from behind the desk.

"What in the world happened, Fred?"

"Oh, nothing," he explained. "Just age. Getting old can be tough sometimes. Speaking of age, remind me of your real name, greenhorn."

"Courtney."

"Yeeeah! That's right! Courtney! Ok, Ms. Courtney, let's take a look at what you got."

We walked outside and I started to open the back of the bed of the truck to show him my table when a man called out from another truck.

"Hey, FRED!" He didn't sound happy.

Fred looked up, "Oh, howdy, Bud."

Bud looked like he was in his sixties and, judging by the frown on his face, might've been baptized at an early age in pickle juice.

Without even acknowledging my presence, Bud started in, "Look here, Fred. This table you sold me won't fit in my living room. After looking at it, it just ain't what I'm looking for. I'd like my money back."

"Well, Bud, you've had the table for two months! If you didn't like it, why didn't you bring it back then?"

"Well, I've been busy. Edna and I just ain't had the time to come over. Besides, you've always made good on other things I don't like. Look here, the table leg is cracked."

"Now, Bud, you and I looked at this table when you bought it. You know that table leg was cracked when you bought it. That's why you got it for only $40," Fred calmly replied. It was almost as if Fred had had this conversation before with Bud.

"I know," said Bud, immediately changing his tune. "But I thought I'd at least ask. So what am I supposed to do about this, Fred? I can't find nothing in there that'll do and Edna ain't gonna be happy when I come home empty handed. She's got to have a table and that wasn't what she was looking for."

I decided to sheepishly step in. "Ummm.... Well I've...." Bud seemed a bit irritated that I dared to speak and interrupt his interruption.

"Yeah, what do you want?" he rudely replied.

I was pretty sure he didn't mean anything by it. It was just his way so I continued, "You said you were looking for a table. I have one here that I was about to sell. It's solid oak and it's been a good table. Would this one work?" I asked pointing to the table in the back of my truck.

Bud surveyed it, rubbing on it and looking underneath from his lower vantage point. "Hmm, how much you asking?" He strongly emphasized, "asking" to inform me that whatever price I named would not be the price I would be getting.

"Well, now, Bud," Fred chimed in, "That there is a family heirloom, so don't try and steal it from her. She'll just get insulted and drive off with some goodies in there I'm needing."

"If it was 'air looms' she wouldn't be selling it! How much you wantin may'um?"

I had been watching closely enough to know what I was in for. I scratched the side of my face and said, "Well... I wanted to get $200 for it. As Fred said, it's a family heirloom."

Immediately Bud shot back, "$100."

"$160" I replied, looking him dead in the eye.

"I might go $110."

I wasn't going to let him win. Ignoring Bud, I looked at Fred and said, "Let's go inside and talk about how much you'll buy this beautiful table for."

I started to close the back of the truck and walk off when Bud chimed back in, "Ok, Ok. Look." He reached in his wallet and pulled out a wad of cash. "All I have is $140. I can't go no higher than that or my wife a' skin me alive. Besides, this here's my poker money!"

I acted as if I still couldn't do it. I didn't say anything but the look on my face said it all.

"Oh, wait!" exclaimed Bud. "I forgot! I have $10 in my glove box in the truck." He ran back to his truck and returned with $10 more and announced, "$150. How about it Air Loom Lady? It's all I got. Take it or leave it."

Still acting reluctant, I took the money and said, "Well, I guess it'll do."

"Good!" Bud said with excitement and the first smile I had seen him give all day.

I started to get the table out of the truck when Fred said, "Hang on, Ms. Courtney. I'll have Joey and Don get that out." They worked with Fred to assist in moving large things around. They loaded the table in Bud's truck. He gave me the cash and drove off.

Fred just stood there and watched him drive off, then turned to me and said, "Well, well. Greenhorn has grown up! That was some good horse trading!"

I turned to Fred and said "Thank you," then I immediately handed him $30.

Confused, Fred asked, "What is this for?"

I smiled and replied, "I actually only wanted $100 for the table, and I did knock you out of a sale. Besides, I enjoyed getting extra for the sale because he was so grouchy."

"Oh, don't mind Bud. It's just his way. He'll be in here again in another few weeks complaining about something else. He don't mean nothing by it. But I gotta tell you, I'm impressed with how you handled him.

"Thanks, Fred. It was fun."

"Truth be told," Fred confided, "I appreciated your help. I can handle 'ol Bud but you just stepped right in and handled that beautifully. Is this all you was here for today or did you want to look around the store for something else?"

I didn't have anything I wanted to buy, but my heart went out to this old man. I think he was lonely and wanted to talk so I said, "I'm not sure. Let's have a look around the store."

We walked inside the store and I looked around. Fred asked, "Are ya' lookin' for anything in particular?"

"Not really. Just lookin," I replied, unconsciously mimicking him. He smiled and said, "Ok, let's go look at stuff."

Fred walked me around the store telling me about various items. It seemed many of them had stories behind them. And even though I didn't want to buy anything, the stories behind the items made them much more appealing.

In a very kind way, Fred asked me about my family. I told him about Bobby and the kids. I joked that my house was a junk store of sorts, too, but I had gotten rid of the clutter and got some things organized there and actually enjoyed the process.

Fred immediately said, "You could help do the same thing here!"

I laughed and replied, "Yeah, right."

Fred laughed then said, "Really, I'm needing some help. Well, you probably got other jobs and things to do, though."

Before thinking, I blurted out, "Not really. But I…"

Fred immediately jumped back in, "I'm looking for some part-time help. Anybody that can handle a guy like Bud can handle this here business. I don't know what all you do during the day, but would you consider working here? Like I said, it'll only be part time. I'll show you the ropes, teach you how this thing works, and I'll even work things around your schedule. Now, come on, you can't beat that!"

I was too stunned to reply. I sat there with my mouth open, searching for an answer. All I managed to get out was, "Uh... I'll… think about it."

"Great!" boomed Fred. "I'll look forward to hearin' from ya'!"

Chapter 20
Facing the Music

I drove home from the antique store and wondered what Bobby and the kids would think about Fred's offer. As I fixed dinner that afternoon, I decided I would bring it up at the table for all of the family to discuss.

At dinner I found the right moment to bring it up when Bobby asked, "So how'd it go at the junk store today? Did you get anything for the table?"

I smiled and proudly placed on the table a wad of one and five dollar bills that looked like it was a thousand dollars. The kids had a ball counting it.

They all "Ooh'd and Ah'd" over my deal and told me how good they thought it was. The look on my face must have told Bobby I had more to talk about though.

"Did something else happen, honey?" he asked.

"Kind of. Yes." I replied. "Remember me telling you about the junk store owner, Fred? You know, he was the kind, funny, older man who gave me that great deal on the trunk. Well, when I saw him today he wasn't feeling very well. I helped him with a few things, then... (I took a breath here)... he asked me if I wanted a part-time job working there."

The kids laughed. My teenager sarcastically said, "Mom! Working for a junk dealer! That's great!" she exclaimed with a roll of her eyes.

Bobby wasn't laughing. I think he could tell I was seriously thinking about it when he asked, "What'd you say?"

"I told him I wanted to talk to you all about it and think about it. Now that the house is decluttered, it pretty much takes care of itself. I have routines in place and I've been wondering what to do in my spare time. It seems like this would be a fit for me. I enjoy the negotiating and I think Fred really needs the help. It's hard to explain, but I think I'm supposed to be there. It won't interfere with my schedule and routines here. It's only part time. I can go in after I drop the kids off at school and I'll get off in plenty of time to pick them up."

"How much does it pay?" asked Bobby.

"We haven't discussed specifics yet," I replied. "I didn't want to go any further until we talked."

By this time the kids had stopped joking. They all realized I was serious.

"Wow, Mom," said Audrey. "I didn't think you were serious about it. Is it something you really want to do?"

"I think I might like it," I replied. "I really enjoyed the work and helping out was an added bonus. I'd at least like to try it. Fred really needs the help. He's already hired people to load and unload things. All I would really be doing is helping Fred run the store and managing the sales."

There was complete silence after my comment and then Bobby finally broke the quiet with, "Well, Lord knows you can manage a sale." We all laughed as he continued, "I think if this is something you really want to try, then you should do it."

I was so happy that my husband was supporting me in this. I'm not sure I could've done it without my family behind me. I still had some doubts, though, and I asked, "What about errands during the day? And there's always the possibility I'll have to work late. We have to be prepared for those times if this is going to work."

The kids immediately chimed in that they would help. (Ok, I had heard that one before when we gave in and bought a puppy but Bobby said he would help too.) Once they all stepped in and agreed to help, it gave me the last push I needed.

I was going to call Fred and tell him I was showing up tomorrow to go over the specifics. I got ahold of him around 8:30 that night. He sounded like he was about to go to sleep. I guess he was tired. I told him I could be there by 9 AM, right after I dropped the kids off at school. His voice perked up and I thought maybe he was as excited as I was.

I had a hard time sleeping that night because I was so excited about my new adventure. The feeling was similar to Christmas Eve when I was a kid. This felt like a whole new chapter in my life.

I pulled up to the store at 8:53 AM. My stomach was in knots. It reminded me of the time I did my school play in 5th grade and had butterflies in my stomach before the curtain opened. It was exciting and sickening all at the same time.

I got out of the car and didn't see Fred outside and walked in the front door to find him. The bell at the top of the door announced my arrival. I still heard nothing. I looked around at the front part of the store. I guess I've never really described what this place looks like so I probably should do that now.

Even though it was a "junk" store, the front of the store certainly didn't seem like one. Everything was where it was supposed to be. There were some beautiful curio cabinets and armoires that lined the walls to my left. You could see they were dusty and older, filled with some wonderful treasures. And you could see that they were right where they should be in the store to capture the whim of just about any buyer. There was something of interest for everyone.

To my right was a wall full of a collection of trunks, antique toys, and Tiffany lamps. In between these walls was furniture of all kinds: couches, chairs, end tables, and desks were arranged in a pattern that allowed a path between all of them. Behind these were some more beveled glass cabinets full of porcelain figurines and collectibles. Some of the cabinets had interior lights that illuminated the treasures. As I walked around the cabinets to the center of the store there was a glass case that had four sides encircling where the cash register was. The cases were filled with necklaces, rings, and jewelry that were valuable estate pieces. Another case was filled with an assortment of knives and the case next to it was stocked with antique watches. I couldn't believe how many were in there! The last case featured some sort of turquoise, silver, and semi precious stone jewelry.

The back half of the store was completely different. It truly lived up to its name. It was a junky potpourri of chairs stacked on top of musty furniture with magazines, books, and clutter pouring from the top. I walked up to one of the recliners that was stacked oddly next to a rattan chair and slapped my hand on the fabric at the top of the recliner. A plume of dust that shot three feet in the air immediately greeted me, adding a dusty odor to the already musty smell of the place.

As I glanced toward the back of the store I could see light peeking in from what was probably a door left open. I stepped through the shafts of light from the upper windows that painted the cluttered mess with dust-filled beams of light until I found the back door. I could see the moving boys talking and laughing. There on an overturned empty paint bucket sat Fred, peeling an apple with a pocketknife.

"Howdy, Ms. Courtney! We're just so proud to have you here today! Ain't we boys? You ready to get going?"

I smiled and announced, "I sure am, Fred."

"Well, good! Come on up to the front," Fred replied as he stood up and walked back in the door. He was moving slowly and it seemed he was in pain, but he never mentioned it. To every customer he was his usual, jovial, boisterous self. I could tell he was hurting though.

We got to the front of the store in time to hear the bell ring. The first customer of the day. It was a middle-aged woman wearing a dress suit. I greeted her warmly. She had a pleasant, business like demeanor. She had an armoire for sale. Her two teenage sons had unloaded it from a truck and were waiting with it outside.

Fred and I walked outside to see it. It was beautiful. It was a really old one and in great shape.

The woman's name was Donna. She explained, "This armoire belonged to my aunt. She just passed away and we don't have room for it. I'd like to sell it."

Fred asked, "You want to sell it outright or consign it?"

"Sell it," Donna replied.

Fred looked at her for a moment and then looked at the armoire. Then he looked at me and announced to Donna, "My associate here handles these things. Ms. Courtney, what do you think about it?"

My mind started spinning. It was a miracle I didn't blurt out, "HUH?" but I'm sure my face had said it loud and clear. I pulled my thoughts together. I had seen many armoires like this in antique stores. I knew, in this condition, they normally sold in other stores from $250 up to $600. I judged this one to be on the higher end of the spectrum.

"It's very nice," I managed to finally say.

"Thank you," Donna replied. I was thinking, "Now what?" Do I offer her a price? I didn't want to insult her but I didn't want to lose money either. Based on my price range of $250 to $600, I offered, "I'd say it's worth about $200 to us."

Immediately Donna replied, "I'll take it!" Both her sons smiled at each other. Fred never said a word.

I was quite pleased with myself. I knew the minimum I could sell it for was $250 and if I found the right person I could get around $500. And sure enough, by the end of the day somebody came in, saw the armoire and asked about it. I had our asking price at $500. Fred let it go for $300! I couldn't believe it! I just knew I could have gotten $400 minimum.

I think he could tell I wasn't pleased with the deal, so he asked me to sit down and go over things for a minute.

"What'd you think about that deal, Courtney?"

"Honestly? I thought we could have done better," I frankly replied.

"Yes, that's some good thinkin. You're exactly right!"

"Then why did you take so little for it?" I asked a bit scolding.

Fred smiled and kindly replied, "Ms. Courtney, there's some method behind this madness."

I jumped in, "But I think I could've gotten $350 or $400 for it."

Fred put his hand up to scratch his chin, then said, "Maybe you could have. But if you did get that you'd have hurt yourself in the long run."

"How so?" I asked.

"You gotta remember that this is a different type of store. People come here looking for deals. And they keep coming back because they got that deal. Ain't that why you came back here?"

I thought about it, smiled, and said, "Yes."

Fred continued very kindly, "You gotta remember: This here is a junk store. People don't come here to pay retail. The whole idea is to get a great deal and when they get that deal they come back here a'lookin' for another one AND they tell their friends too. You understand what I'm saying?"

Fred smiled knowing I understood we weren't there to make a killing but make a good deal for everyone. I smiled back and said, "I understand. But you agreed that we could've done better. How could we have done better?"

Fred leaned back in his chair and then said, "Now, Ms. Courtney, you know I like you. I have since the first day you walked in here. I feel like you got talent to do this business." I sensed there was a "but" coming. "But... we coulda bought that armoire for a lot less. Probably $100 less."

"Really?" I wondered about that when they jumped at my first offer. "I'm so sorry."

"It's ok. No need to apologize. I'm the one that threw you in the deep end of the water cause I wanted to see what you could do. And we still made a profit and that's the bottom line. But I want you to remember the first rule of negotiating: Whoever says the first number has the disadvantage. Let the other person say how much they want to sell it for or how much they're willing to give for something. Always let them say it first. You'll be surprised at what people want. Sometimes it is too much, but many times it's way less than you think it will be."

Fred reassured me when he said, "We win some and we lose some and this one was still a win." I was much more cautious as the next customer came in. They had some figurines for sale.

I happened to know about this set of figurines because my daughter, Audrey, had collected them when she was in elementary school. The set this lady was selling was a complete set in mint condition and could bring as much as $350 to the right collector. I was about to mention this to Fred when he whispered to me, "That's a complete collection and it's in mint condition."

I was astounded at how much Fred knew. I guess in this business you have to know a lot about all sorts of things. It made me realize how much I had to learn and how lucky I was to have Fred to teach me. For all of his rough and disarming exterior, he truly was a shrewd businessman. Remembering the lesson I had just learned, I didn't say a word. I sat there and watched him work.

"Ok, is this all you have for me to look at today?" Fred asked.

"Yes, it is. This set belonged to my daughter. She left for college last month and said for me to get rid of the kiddy stuff. I thought some little girl might like to have these."

"Alright," Fred smiled as he asked, "How much you wantin for them?"

"I'm not really sure," she replied. "How much will you give me for them?"

It was like watching a game of chess. Fred never wavered though, "Now, I'm sure you came in here with a price in mind. Why don't you tell me how much you were a'wanting?" His manner was so disarming. I couldn't match that, but I thought I could be disarming in a different way.

"Well, I was just cleaning things out. Does $50 sound fair?"

I was ready to scream out "TAKE IT! TAKE IT! TAKE IT!" but Fred didn't budge. He looked at the figurines thoughtfully and then with a scratch of his chin he said in a begrudging tone, "Yeah. I could do $50." And with that, the deal was done. Amazing! Absolutely amazing to watch his calm demeanor in negotiating.

The lady left the store with a smile on her face, as happy as she could be. I told Fred how amazed I was at the deal he got. He just smiled back and said, "I told ya' you'd be surprised."

"That set is worth nearly $350!" I excitedly informed.

"Well, that may be what it's worth, but remember. It ain't just about what it's worth. It's what you can get somebody to pay for it. You can buy a $1000 couch for $10 but if there ain't no buyer it's still a loss. You gotta know what people will buy and what they won't."

Confused, I asked, "But that's such a specialty item, how do you know you'll find a buyer for that?"

Fred pointed below the counter and said, "Hand me that notebook." I looked under the counter and saw an old notebook that looked like a three-ring binder from the '70s. Fred ran his finger down the tabs. The tabs in the notebook reminded me of my FlyLady Control Journal.

He settled on one tab and flipped the notebook open. The handwritten title at the top read, "Items people are looking for." He scanned down the list and came to one entry that read, "Pretty Girl Figurines Complete Set." Next to the entry was a date, a name and a phone number. Fred picked up the phone and when the other line picked up said, "Howdy, Ms. Amy. This is Fred from the antique store. You was in here two months ago looking for that 'Pretty Girl Figurine Set.' Did you ever find one?" He paused to listen, then smiled and said, "Yes ma'am. I sure did. I got it right here. You wanna come by and look at it? Yes, ma'am. We'll be here til 6. See you then."

He already had buyers lined up! He ended up selling that set to Amy for $200. He could've gotten more but I was beginning to see what he was talking about. Amy was thrilled to get that set for $200 and Fred made a huge profit! She gave Fred a list of things she was looking for and asked him to call as soon as he found it. She was definitely a satisfied customer. She also mentioned she had some old bookcases and chairs she didn't need anymore and wondered if he could sell them for her.

Before I knew it, it was almost time for me to get the kids. I was about to leave when Fred said, "Here, Ms. Courtney. Before you go, we gotta enter these receipts." He pulled a stack of receipts out of the drawer and began to sort them out.

"Do you do these every day, Fred?"

"Oh, yeah! You gotta! If you don't do this, then you don't really know where you stand. You gotta balance out these receipts. There's nothing worse for a person in business to do than ignore where they stand financially. That's a short road to a quick death."

Conviction was setting in as I thought about how bad I was with finances. There were many times I wouldn't even look at the bills. In my mind, ignorance was bliss. I saw that was a wrong attitude. I thought about my "secret credit card" that I kept hidden from Bobby. I knew I had to work on this area in a big way, especially if I was going to help run a business.

Fred finished counting the receipts and we entered them into the computer in the back office. In spite of the disorganization of his office, he had the essentials down to a science.

As I drove to pick up the kids from school, I thought about the financial side of my life. My forgetfulness in paying bills had caused our water to be turned off that time. I had decluttered my house and blessed it, but I hadn't blessed my finances. Not by a long shot. I knew FlyLady had some information on it. I decided it was high time I looked it up when I got home.

When I got home and got the kids situated, I went to the computer and pulled up FlyLady's website and found her information on finances. It spelled out an acronym: FACE.

"Financial Awareness Continually Empowers." Now isn't that so clever? How in the world did she find ways to make finances fun? I had been the most financially unaware person I could possibly be which, for a college accounting major, was embarrassing. I had to "face the music" as the saying goes. It was time to look at my finances.

FlyLady had some forms I downloaded from her website that helped me remember all the monthly bills I had. In order to do this, though, I had to go through the same process that Fred had done at the store. I had to have receipts. I started my scavenger hunt. I found receipts on the floorboard of my car, in my purse, in the desk, on the counter tops, some were in bags in the trash, and some were just gone.

I called the bank and got my balance. I knew it should match mine but I didn't really have a balance so just started with their amount and went from there. I kept remembering FlyLady's encouragement to just jump in where I was so that's what I did. I kept telling myself, "I'm not behind. I'm not behind."

By the time I had gone through everything it wasn't pretty. I had some work to do here. Don't get me wrong. Bobby made good money, but we didn't have the time to go through all the bills together. That was supposed to be my job. I hadn't done a very good job of it and my "hidden" credit card seemed even more wrong. I decided to come clean with Bobby that night. The balance on that card was... well... let's just say it was a LOT and leave it at that. I thought I could earn it at the store in a few months.

I decided to go over everything with Bobby about our finances. I told him where we were. He was surprised. When I told him about the credit card, he didn't say much. I could tell he was hurt that I had kept it from him though. I had damaged his trust in me. Then he apologized to me for not taking a more active role in our finances. Talk about feeling bad, I felt bad enough already. Facing my finances wasn't fun, BUT I felt so much better at least knowing where we were so we could take steps to correct the problem.

I thought I wouldn't sleep well that night but I actually did. Telling the truth lifted a great weight from my shoulders. I wondered if our trust could be rebuilt. The next morning before he left for work he told me he loved me. It wasn't in his usual strong voice, but I knew he meant it. I fixed his favorite meal that night. When he got home from work, he brought me flowers. I think that was his way of saying all was forgiven, but I was still going overboard to rebuild his trust in me.

From that point on we did our finances together. I also found a great way to organize my receipts in my Control Journal. FlyLady had so many great resources to help me get all this done. One of the things that astounded me was how much money I was spending on eating out and spontaneous trips to the grocery store. It was the bleeding artery of our finances. I had to stop the bleeding immediately.

At first the kids really whined about not eating out. How spoiled we had become! I put the FlyLady rule, "NO WHINING ALLOWED!" on the refrigerator. Menu Planning became even more key in our system. It wasn't just about the food now. It was about financial well-being. Spontaneous buying was killing our budget. There were other cuts we made, too. We realized that our cable TV expanded channels weren't really benefiting us. We rarely watched them. Bobby and I decided to do away with that and go with the basic ones. That cut another $80 from our budget. I actually found a lot of ways to trim our expenses through the ideas on the FlyLady website. I found out that decluttering my finances was similar to everything else. It took patience and Baby Steps but with continued work came progress. The key was being aware and "FACEing" my finances.

At the antique shop, I had learned to organize the receipts for Fred. I was entering them in the computer for him. The program was very user friendly and took no time at all to learn. Speaking of organizing, the back half of the store was next on my "project" list. I started decluttering the store. It's kind of funny thinking about decluttering a store whose business is "clutter" but I was able to get Fred to realize that some things just didn't need to stay on the sales floor.

It took the helpers several trips to the city dump but before long the back half of the store looked as good as the front half. I still didn't understand why the front and the back were different from each other. But, oh well, it was all pretty now.

After three months, the store was looking good and lots of new customers were flowing in. I was learning more and more about "making the deals" as Fred called it. I did pretty well on most of them but there were a few I lost on. They weren't major (just a couple of hundred dollars total) but they were big lessons for me. The good news was I was learning from my mistakes. As many as I was making it was a wonder I wasn't a genius yet, but Fred took it all in good humor.

Fred was always telling me what a great job I was doing. It gave me the encouragement to keep going. I noticed he continued to struggle with getting around the store. I asked him about it every now and then and he would just say the same thing, "Just age. Just age." I also noticed how pleased he was at the overall business revenue. I had nothing to compare it to, but Fred's countenance clearly seemed to say things were going very well.

In four months, we had some really wonderful pieces in the store. I knew they were going to do well and create some big revenue for Fred and the store. I also had knocked my credit card down by HALF! I was halfway home. Consistently facing my finances was really working.

I wanted to help Fred declutter his office but he gently replied, "Now, Little 'Un (he had dropped the 'Ms. Courtney' by now) everything has its place in there. When you've been in the same room for 43 years, you know where everything is. Cleaning it would be like starting over again for me and I'm just too far along to do that."

I thought I could help him but I never pressed the issue. I wanted to help him. The more I worked in the store, the more I was learning about the business and I was also learning there was a lot more to me than I realized. Bobby and the kids commented on the difference in me. I was thankful I had gotten the courage to FACE the things in my life that I needed to face.... especially fear!

I began to believe in and have confidence in myself in the business.

Chapter 21
Finishing Well

Two months later, I was driving to the store one morning. I was thinking about how good it felt to have that credit card completely paid off. It was such a feeling of satisfaction. A feeling like chains that were around my neck were now lying at my feet. I was anticipating the time I was spending at the store. It was fun every day. At least normally it was.

I got to the store a little bit late because one of the teachers in the car line needed to talk to me. She asked me to volunteer for the PTA and help out in the classroom a few times a month. My normal response would have been "Sure I can!" but with this new job I knew I couldn't.

I always worried about telling people "no." I was scared they wouldn't like me. I politely but apprehensively replied, "I'm honored you would ask, but with my responsibilities at the antique store and my family, I wouldn't be able to give you a full commitment and really wouldn't do a good job. My family has to come first."

The teacher replied, "I wish other parents would feel the same way and not give a halfhearted commitment."

I was impressed! She didn't reject me. In fact, she respected me more! My "no" had actually worked!

I drove to the store. When I walked in the door, I knew something was wrong because Joey was there to greet me.

"What's wrong?" I intensely asked.

"It's Fred," Joey replied, "He collapsed this morning."

"Oh my gosh!"

"He's ok. He just had a fainting spell. He's evidently been sick for a while. The doctor said it might be pneumonia."

"Oh, my goodness! That's awful! I've got to get down there. Is he at the downtown hospital?"

Joey interrupted, "He told me to tell you he wanted you to stay here and mind the store and that he was counting on you.'

"But who is going to take care of him?" I pleaded.

"He has a close family friend. They're already there. Fred asked you to take care of things here. He said you would know what to do."

I thought about it. I really wanted to be there at the hospital to check on Fred, but he did need me here. Then it suddenly set in that I would be doing everything by myself. I had been doing most things by myself but I always had Fred there as my "safety net" and now… it was all up to me.

The thoughts of all this caused me to be nervous, but I remembered after I first came here, Fred and I made a list. I went to my car and found a notebook I had made and, sure enough, there was my list. This book was a miniature version of my Control Journal at home. I just made it for my work. It gave me comfort and confidence.

The first day went by smoothly. We only had a few customers, which I know isn't good for business, but it suited me just fine. I added up the receipts and closed early so I could get the kids. As soon as Bobby was home I went to the hospital. Fred wasn't there. I asked for more information but they couldn't give me any more information than telling me Fred had gone home. I had no clue where he lived so I called his home number.

A woman picked up the phone, "Hello, Fred Palmer's residence."

"Yes," I answered, "This is Courtney Harrison. I was calling to check on Fred."

"Oh, yes! Courtney from the store! Well, the good news is, it isn't pneumonia. His lungs are clear. The bad news is the doctor said he has to rest for at least four days. After that he should be fine. He just had a bit of an inner ear infection that caused the dizziness. He's actually wanting to be at the store tomorrow but I'm going to keep him here. My son and I are keeping him company."

"I'm sorry", she said. "Where are my manners? I'm Baby, a close friend of the family."

Baby? Fred had talked about Baby before in conversations. She evidently meant a great deal to Fred and his wife.

"Yes, he talks about you all the time. I feel like I already know you. How's Fred? Is he awake?"

"No," she replied, "he's sleeping right now. They gave him quite a bit of medicine."

"Ok. Please tell him I'll handle the store for this week. He doesn't need to come in. Just get better."

"I'll tell him," she replied. "You should know he speaks so highly of you. He says you have breathed new life into the store.

He loves that place and for him to say that is really saying something. I'm sure you'll be just fine on your own this week."

"Thank you," I sincerely replied. "Please take care of him. He's such a sweet man."

"Don't worry about him. He'll be good as new in a few days." And with that, we hung up the phone.

I was grateful for the light day because the rest of the day was extremely busy. I actually preferred it that way, though, because the hours passed quicker when I was busy. I was able to sell a dining room set for a large profit. I knew Fred would like that.

I counted my receipts every day and at the end of the week I ran payroll (which was a new one for me) and updated the inventory list. By the end of the week I realized Fred was right. I was just fine. I could do this job and I was really enjoying it.

It was fun helping people who came in wanting something. I enjoyed creating a situation where they got what they wanted, we got what we needed, and the next person got what they wanted. Everybody got a bargain, which is exactly what Fred wanted. It was as if I had become a professional problem solver. Deep inside I felt this was what I was meant to do.

Fred got back to the store on Saturday afternoon. That was usually a very busy time for us. I was taking care of customers when he came in. I asked if he had driven himself and he had. I was a little perturbed by this because I thought Baby was taking care of him. When I asked where she was, Fred told me she had gone back home but he was fine. He looked tired, but other than that he was his old self. He shooed me away to take care of the customers.

Bobby and I worked it out so he could pick up the kids and I could stay until closing to help Fred. Fred didn't do a lot that day except sit on a stool and talk with all the customers. I'm pretty sure that many customers came to the store to socialize with Fred and reminisce about old times and hear him spin a wonderful story. He never disappointed. He was his usual friendly self, talking to everyone, never meeting a stranger, but it was easy to see he was very tired. I tried to encourage him to go home and rest but he said he needed to be there. I wasn't sure why.

He was watching me interact with the customers. I could be mistaken, but I had grown better at reading Fred. I would describe the look on his face as pride. I would return to the counter with the receipts. He would occasionally encourage me and say, "Great deal!" or "Good job."

The day continued steadily until quitting time. I picked up the receipts to go to the back and add them up. Fred followed me to the back and pulled the office door closed and said he needed to talk to me. He had never done anything like that before. I felt uneasy so I asked, "Is everything ok? Have I done something wrong?"

"Oh, no, Courtney!" he assured. "But I do need to talk to you. He opened his wallet and pulled out a photo and handed it to me. The photo looked like it was taken in the '60s. It was of a beautiful couple. I could tell from the smile on the man's face that it was Fred. The woman had dark hair, but since the picture was black and white I couldn't tell the color. Her eyes sparkled and her face told you she was a kind person. The photographer seemed to have caught a wonderful moment because the woman was laughing. Her face beamed with joy and happiness.

"Is this you and your wife?" I asked.

"That's my Martha," he answered with a look of admiration. "That picture was taken not too long after we started the store. They actually printed it in the newspaper and did a little article about us. We was so excited about starting out." Fred's smile dimmed to a more thoughtful look as he continued, "We had a great life together. We laughed and loved a lot."

"Do you mind if I ask what happened to her?"

After a pause he replied, "Cancer. It was the weirdest thing. She never smoked or drank a day in her life, but that thing got her. Some things you just don't understand." His eyes were becoming misty now. So were mine.

"There ain't a day that goes by that I don't miss her. Me and her was partners in life. And a big part of our life together was this here business. When she was gone, I didn't know if I could ever continue. I just kind of limped along. But since you got here, things have picked up."

I wanted to ask what he meant, but I didn't want to interrupt. He was choked up and so was I. After several seconds of silence he continued, "Courtney, I'm just a'gonna shoot it straight to you. I'm too old to do this business anymore and since Martha's gone, my heart just ain't in it no more like it was. My body can't keep up with this. I'm eighty-four years old and I can't do it."

EIGHTY-FOUR? I would never have known he was that old. Maybe seventy, but never eighty-four!

Fred continued, "I don't have any family to pass it along to. Martha and me never could have no kids. This here place really is our baby and I can't just let anybody take it. But you're not just anybody. I think you're the right person to take it."

"Take it? You mean you're going to sell this place?"

"Yes, ma'am, I do. But not to just anyone. I want to sell this store to you. I think you could take this whole business and do it better than anyone else could. You got the instincts for it and you know the business now. You've gotten real good with the money side. You organized the store and sales started booming. I'm telling you, Courtney. You can do it."

"But, Fred, I couldn't afford to buy this from you, I don't have the money to just..."

"Now, Courtney," he interrupted, "I've already figured that out. Listen, I've got more money now than I need for the rest of my life. This thing has paid me pretty well." He pulled out an envelope and continued, "I figured you might have a concern about the money so I thought I'd finance it for you. I own this property outright, so there's no mortgage to apply for. All you need to do is figure if you want to do it."

"Well, how much would I have to pay every month?" He told me the amount. It sounded so .huge. I stammered, "Uhhhhh, Fred! I don't know that I could ever..."

Again he calmly interrupted, "Hold on, hold on,'" He walked back through the door and led me to the counter. He pulled a ledger from underneath and said, "Look here." I looked over his shoulder at the receipts. I had only entered them. I had no idea this business generated so much income!

"I didn't know it made that much profit every month!"

Fred smiled, "The truth is, Courtney, it hasn't since Martha passed on. In the last seven months we've seen a HUGE increase in income." Leaning forward for emphasis he continued, "The last seven months since you been here, the business has been growing by bucket loads. You were made to do this here business. You're a natural. The customers love you. They keep coming back and bringing all their friends with them. You're a magnet… just like my Martha was."

"I have to admit, the last seven months have really been fantastic. I've felt like I've been doing what I was supposed to be doing all along. It's as if I've finally found my purpose. I enjoy putting these deals together and helping people find things they've always wanted. It's like I'm making people's dreams come true. It's been wonderful."

"Like I said," Fred continued, handing me the envelope, "You was made for this. Take that envelope to your husband, and you and him let an accountant and a lawyer look it over. They'll tell you what kind of deal you're getting. I've included several years of financial statements and they're current up to this month. You give this some thought and get back with me, ok?"

"So let me get this straight. If I sign whatever's in here, I'll own this place?"

"Yep, you got it." Fred replied very matter-of-factly.

I went home that night and told Bobby what had happened. I told him how nervous I was about it. We looked over the paperwork together. Fred was selling me the store and the land it was on. I thought it was just a lease but it wasn't. And the price he was giving it to me for was about half of what it was worth! After checking it out with our accountant and a lawyer, they confirmed that it was a spectacular deal.

I told Fred I wanted a week to think it over. As the week went on it turned out to be the biggest revenue week we'd ever had. Fred said it was the biggest week he'd ever seen!

Bobby and I decided to take the offer. It was a big leap for us but I knew we could do it. I walked into the store in the morning and proudly announced, "Fred, Bobby and I have talked it over and we've decided this is an offer we can't refuse. We've decided to accept your gift and take your offer! Here are the signed papers."

"That's great!!" Fred bellowed and laughed. "We'll get this going. By the way, Baby's coming into town at the end of the week to help me move."

"MOVE? You're moving? I thought you were staying here to help! You're just going to abandon me???"

"Now, Little 'Un, this store is yours. You don't need my help. You can do it. I gotta move my stuff out. This is your space now. That's why Baby's coming to help me move."

"She doesn't have to do that. I can help you."

"Don't you worry about that. I got plenty to keep us busy for the next week until she gets here. I got a big project for us to work on for the rest of this week."

It wasn't normal for Fred to assign me a project. "What project is that?" I curiously asked.

Fred smiled at me with that big, broad, familiar, wise smile and then replied, "Something you've been a'hankering to do for a while. Clean out my office."

Chapter 22
Purpose and People

Fred's office was a piece of work. It smelled of musty papers and something else I couldn't quite put my finger on. In the corner were two gray metal filing cabinets that were peppered with dents. There were mountains of papers and files on top of the cabinets that nearly reached the eight-foot ceiling. The second file cabinet partially covered the only window in the office. It's not as if it mattered, because the window was so stained you couldn't see through it anyway. In every corner of the room were stacks of boxes with papers spilling out of the top. Each stack was at least four feet tall.

Next to the wall opposite of the filing cabinets were two chairs. One was a cloth-covered beige wooden chair. The fabric was torn on the armrest and the seat. The other chair was a leather club chair that was in decent condition other than the one tear in the cushion and a few scratches on the side. It seemed so out of place. Fred mostly sat in this chair. I think it was "his."

The centerpiece of the office was an old gray metal desk. Behind the desk was an old black office chair that was apparently broken because the backrest was leaning off to the right and one armrest was just hanging. In the chair was a stack of files. One leg of the metal desk was attached with duct tape. There was a calendar on the desk from three years ago that had scribbles written all over it. It was barely visible though because of the 13 different stacks (yes, I counted) of papers intermixed with a hodgepodge of magazines, newspapers, Kleenex boxes, mail (both opened and unopened) and a few empty, crumpled up fast food bags. There was a large brown trashcan next to the desk which was, ironically, empty. This was going to take some time.

Fred chimed in, "Now, I know it looks a mess, but believe it or not, I know where everything is in here. I keep all my files from years past over here." He was pointing to the boxes in the corner with the papers flowing out of them. Upon closer inspection I could barely see that he had taken a ballpoint pen and written dates on the sides of the brown boxes.

"The desk has stuff I'm currently working on, and the chair behind the desk is the stuff for this week," he continued, "and the top drawer of this here file cabinet (it was the one partially covering the window) has all the receipts for this year. I always keep them right in here."

I was smiling and nodding while thinking, "This is going to take some MAJOR organizational skills to accomplish."

"What about the other file cabinet?" I asked.

Fred stopped for a second and his facial expression changed. I had touched a nerve. After pausing he replied, "That there was Martha's stuff. I can't hardly go through it. I suppose that's why I kinda let this thing go like I have. But like I said, I know where MOST everything is. After I seen you organize the rest of the store out there, I knew this little office wouldn't be no problem for you."

"I'll help you, Fred. Don't worry," I reassured. "Just let me get my pad and I'll start breaking this down."

"I don't think we can get much done this week in here," Fred said.

I had to ask, "How much of this do you want to throw away?"

He gave me permission to throw away anything with the exception of ledger books from previous years and, of course, Martha's stuff in the file cabinet. Having this information let me know how to proceed.

"You'll be surprised." I assured Fred. "It just takes a few Baby Steps to get going in the right direction. Once we get a little momentum, you won't recognize this place."

Monday was usually a slow day so I had quite a bit of time to focus on the office. On my list I had written down the things that needed to go: The broken chairs, the boxes full of papers from 20 years ago that we didn't need, and of course the magazines and newspapers were history. Looking around the office, I see what Fred meant: he knew where everything was because all the clutter was in a stack that related to what was needed.

During my lunch break I went online and reviewed the FlyLady paper clutter section. It had been a while since I had read it so reviewing was a good thing. I dove into the office that afternoon between customers. I had Joey and Don helping me take things to the dumpster. In one afternoon you could already see the progress. I asked Fred if there was any emotional attachment to the old desk. He replied, "Shoot, naw." No doubt, that thing was out of there, too. I went through the drawers with great "fear and trepidation" like I was Indiana Jones going through a cave waiting for creatures to jump out of the dark. It was mostly old pens and papers. Nothing important.

I continued this process for the next four days. It was really looking good by the time Thursday afternoon rolled around. Pretty much everything was decluttered and the dilapidated furniture pieces removed. All that was left was Martha's filing cabinet. I had purposefully saved it for the last thing. I had never even looked in there the entire time I worked here.

I opened up the bottom cabinets. To my surprise there wasn't much in there. There were a few ledger books from years past. The handwriting was much too clear to be Fred's so I assumed they were done by Martha. I smiled at a few of the entries because Fred and Martha would write silly little notes to each other in the ledgers themselves! It looked like they had a fun marriage.

The top drawer is where I encountered what Fred had trouble with. There was a photo album in the drawer stuffed with photos that had spilled out into the bottom of the drawer. I carefully removed the book and photos. This would have made a great photo album but none of the pictures were attached or in the slipcases. They were just generally thrown in there.

Suddenly I heard Fred's voice behind me, "Those are all the pictures I brought from home. I just bought that album and put 'em in there. I was thinking sometime I might be able to organize it into something, but it just never happened."

I asked Fred if he wanted to look through the pictures with me but he politely said, "No. Not right now." I could tell this part was particularly painful for him. Most of the pictures were of Fred and Martha from years gone by. They were such a cute couple and it seemed from the photographs that they truly had a wonderful lifetime of special memories together.

One photo caught my eye. It was slid backwards into the front pocket and the date stamped on the back of the photo told me it was only four years old. I flipped it over and saw Fred, Martha, and a young woman with them. "Who is this with you and Martha, Fred? Is it your daughter? No, wait. You and Martha didn't have kids. You told me that. Who is this?"

"That's Baby. She came in to do some trading, kinda like you, and just became a regular customer. When Martha started falling ill and stayed a spell at the hospital, Baby was volunteering there. She stepped in and became a good friend to Martha, visiting her in the hospital and coming around here to help out."

"It sounds like she kind of was a daughter to you-all."

"I suppose she's the closest thing we ever had to a child, besides this place."

I had to ask, "Fred: why didn't you offer this business to Baby?"

Fred replied, "Well, I thought for a while that I might actually offer it to her, but the more we got to know her, Martha and I knew this just wasn't her cup of tea. Besides, Baby didn't have the knack for this type of thing like you do. She's great with people, but she wouldn't be good at putting the deals together like you. Besides, her heart just wasn't in it. Like you said, it's about purpose. This here place wasn't her purpose, but it is yours."

Fred continued, "You think this place was a mess when you got here? You shoulda seen it before Baby started helping. Martha was the best woman a man could ever have, but she wasn't too good on the organization part. It used to drive her crazy. I'm telling you, Baby stepped in and helped Martha learn all about how to clean up this stuff. She even gave her a book to help her learn to do it. Martha loved that book. She said applying the things from that book gave her peace in so many areas of her life. It taught her how to break down big projects into small pieces. She was gonna organize the whole thing but she got too sick to do it. She was only able to finish the front of the store."

That explained why the front looked so different. I put my hand on Fred's shoulder and said, "Baby sounds like a great friend to you and Martha."

"She's one of the best I know," Fred thoughtfully replied.

"Ok, Fred, I have to ask. Why do you call her 'Baby? Is that her real name?"

Fred laughed, "Oh, Martha started calling her 'Baby doll' and I guess the name just stuck. She's always been so good to us." Pausing for a moment, Fred continued, "When Martha passed on, Baby was there. She helped so much."

A tear started welling up in Fred's eye. "Right before Martha passed on she made Baby promise her two things," and holding up a finger for each one he said, "That she would help me move when it came time for me to let go of the store."

"And what was the second promise?"

Holding up two fingers, Fred replied, "That she would help take care of me when I couldn't take care of myself no more. Like you said, she really is the daughter we never had."

After a pause I said, "I can't wait to meet her."

Fred smiled for a moment, but he wasn't looking at me. He was looking down at the photos laid out on the floor. It was as if he was surveying his life and replaying a precious movie in his mind filled with the best memories a human being could have. He was lost in the moment. I didn't say another word. Some things are just sacred. I kept sorting pictures.

It was then that I found it. It was taped to the back of one of Martha's filing cabinets. It was an envelope made out to Fred from Martha. I carefully peeled it off the back of the filing cabinet. It was sealed. I looked over at Fred. This was far too personal for me to ever look at.

"What is it?" Fred asked.

I simply replied, "It's for you."

Fred immediately recognized the writing and looked back at me with a sort of shocked look. "I'll just step outside." I walked out of the room. The door didn't shut all the way. I went outside the office to help Joey with a customer, but my attention wasn't there. I glanced back through the cracked door to see Fred sitting in a chair and silently crying as he read the letter. Although I wanted to know what it said, I knew there was no way I could ask him. I couldn't invade his privacy like that.

About 20 minutes later, Fred stuck his head out of the office door and called me to come back in.

"Are you ok?" I sincerely asked.

He paused for a moment then replied, "Yeah. I'm fine." I continued working on the office and got it finished. I know that had to have been a difficult moment for Fred, but something in his eyes told me that it was a moment of healing, too.

We had a few customers come in with items that kept us busy for the rest of the day. Fred didn't say too much. I think the whole situation of life and memories was weighing him down. Before I left for home I hugged him. All he said was, "Take care, Little 'Un."

I talked to Bobby that night about the day and about Baby. I felt so awful for Fred. What could we do? I didn't sleep very well because I was worried about Fred and nervous about meeting Baby the next day. I woke up early, got the kids to school and arrived at the store 30 minutes earlier than usual.

Joey walked past me and noticed, "Look at you! All dolled up today!" I did go a little further than normal in my dress, but it felt special and I thought this day deserved a little more than usual. I wanted to look my best because this was going to be Fred's last day at work.

The day went on with many customers. Fridays and Saturdays were really busy days. I was closing out a few receipts for Fred and entering them in the computer when I heard the bell attached to the front door ring out and a young woman's voice call out, "Fred?"

"Baby!" came his booming reply.

It was time to finally meet her.

I came around from the back to see an attractive woman wearing a black dress that strikingly contrasted with her sassy bobbed hair. Her makeup was subtle, but accented everything perfectly. She had warm brown eyes and a smile that was inviting. She gave Fred a big bear hug.

Fred turned around and saw me and said, "Baby, this is her. This is the one I been telling you about. This is Courtney. Courtney, this is mine and Martha's 'Baby Doll.'"

I extended my hand, "Nice to meet you."

Baby said, "I've heard so much about you. Fred has been so pleased with all you've been doing."

"Thanks," I replied. "He's a special man."

"I agree," Baby smiled.

"So, uh, Baby," it felt awkward calling her that!

She sensed it and said with a smile, "Actually, the only person in this world that calls me Baby is Fred. Please call me Gina."

I said, "Oh, ok. Nice to meet you Gina." "Gina?" I thought to myself. Hmm. What a coincidence. Same name as the woman in the diary.

Fred took her back to his office first and then showed her around the store. She was very complimentary of how the store was arranged and organized and Fred graciously gave me complete credit for that. It made me feel very good. Fred and Gina continued their tour while I sat behind the counter.

When they got to the front of the store they were looking at all the trunks when Gina commented, "Look, Fred! This looks just like the trunk I sold to you and Martha all those years ago. Whatever happened to that one?"

With a smile, Fred replied, "I sold it to her. I also gave her 'The Books,'" he said with a wink.

Then it hit me. GINA? This is THE Gina? The Gina from THE DIARY! Oh, my gosh!

Unconsciously my mouth was open and my eyes widened. I walked from behind the counter and looked at Gina and Fred.

Fred gave me that wise old smile that I had seen hundreds of times, "Yes, Courtney. This is Gina from your diary. Like I told you, she and Martha became good friends. Gina helped her organize and... what's that word you always called it?"

"Declutter." Gina answered.

"Yeah! Declutter. You see, we got to know Gina when she brought in that trunk. She and Martha hit it off and when Gina began to help Martha she gave her two books. It was her diary and a book by the Fly something or other..."

"FlyLady!" Gina reminded and giggled.

"Yeah, FlyLady. Well, Martha read that thing day and night. She loved it. It helped her get ahold of some organizational stuff that she hadn't been able to do. The last year of our lives together, she was decluttering everything. Like I said, it gave her peace like I hadn't seen her have before. Martha was overwhelmed by how much of Gina's life she shared in this diary and that she would actually share that information with somebody. Right before Martha died, she made me promise that I give that diary to somebody special. I held onto the books and the trunk for nearly three years. I didn't know if I would ever give it away. And then I met you, Courtney."

I was completely overwhelmed.

Fred continued, "From the moment I met you something inside me told me you was the one. That's the reason I wanted you to get that trunk. I slipped the diary and that 'Fly' book into the trunk when you wasn't looking. Somehow I knew it would be in good hands with you, and I was right. You coming back in here and the job you've been doing with this place, all that wasn't chance. You've proved that you was the one. And now you found your purpose and you're ready to FLY."

I managed to squeak out, "Thank you."

I looked at Gina who was smiling at me and with tears in my eyes said, "Thank you for sharing your life. It has made a difference in mine."

"I'm so glad," she beamed. I sat there for a moment, stunned at what had just happened. I was amazed at the path of life for all of us. I was grateful that my path had intersected theirs. All of these coincidences definitely had been "God Breezes."

I blurted out, "I have to ask you, Gina. How are your husband and the kids doing?" I know it was a personal question, but I felt like Gina was an intimate friend of mine. After all, she'd been a part of my life for so long.

She laughed and said, "Great! Brittany is in college now. She's doing well. She was going to go several hours away but decided to go to a local college so she could stay close to home. Karly is in her first year in high school and loving it. She's involved in all kinds of activities. Ethan is on the middle school football team. He still keeps us all laughing. Dan actually took early retirement from the company and we get to travel together now."

"That's wonderful! What about Susan?"

"Susan and her husband are great. We're still close friends. We even take trips together once a year. Last year we took a cruise."

"Are you still teaching?"

"Absolutely. I love it. It's my purpose in life. I'm not at the school but I tutor students privately every semester. It still gives me time to travel with Dan and it fulfills a great need in my life. I've been able to find joy in all I do."

"But I'd rather hear about you, Courtney." She continued, "I feel like I know you through Fred, but I'd love to hear about you."

I sat there talking to Gina for another hour. I called Bobby and the kids and had them come over and meet her. The whole day was a bit surreal. As the day turned to night and the sun set, the time came for Fred and Gina to leave.

Gina hugged me and said, "It was nice meeting you. Don't worry about Fred. I'll keep my promise to Martha. He's in good hands."

"The best," I replied. "Thank you for... everything."

She smiled and said, "My pleasure."

Fred hugged me and said, "Ok, Ms. Courtney, it's all yours. Truthfully, it's been yours for a while now though. Take it and make it your dream place. DREAM BIG!"

"I will, Fred," I said as I hugged him again. I looked at him and Gina and said, "Thank you for the lessons, the store... and the diary. Finally, I'm finding joy in all that I do, too."

Fred smiled and looked at Gina and replied, "My pleasure."

I had told Bobby to bring the diary with him. I handed it to Gina and thanked her again. She handed the diary back to me and instructed, "It's not mine anymore, Courtney. The diary is now yours to pass along to the next person you feel will benefit from it. It's your responsibility. Pass on what you've been given. Just like the FlyLady did. It's our gift to her for being brave enough to help us."

"I will," I replied with a smile.

I stepped outside with my family to watch Gina and Fred. As Fred was getting in the car, he paused to look at the store one more time. A faint smile spread across his weather beaten face and then he got in the car. Before they drove off, Fred rolled down the window and said, "I left you a note in your desk drawer." He smiled at me with his wise old grin and then they drove off.

I watched them leave. Bobby hugged me and told me he was proud of me. To tell you the truth, I was too.

Bobby and the kids went home. I walked back to my newly cleaned and furnished office, sat in my chair, and opened the desk drawer. There was a large beige envelope with my name on it in Fred's writing. I opened the envelope and dumped out the contents onto the desk. They fell next to the FlyLady book and the diary. There were only three things in the envelope: a folded note from Fred to me, five stapled pages with lists on them, and the letter Martha had written to Fred!

I was a bit shocked that Fred had given something so precious to me. I read Fred's note first:

> *Dear Ms. Courtney,*
>
> *I know you're probably thinking I shouldn't give you the letter from Martha but when you read it I think you'll understand. DREAM BIG!*
>
> *Your friend and fan, Fred*

I picked up the envelope and took out the letter. It was only one page, handwritten by Martha to Fred.

My dearest Fred,

I left this note for you to find after I'm gone. First of all, I want to thank you for loving me all these years. My life with you has been a wonderful adventure and I've loved every minute of it. Secondly, my guess is: If you (or somebody else) found this, then that must mean you've sold the store. I know you made a wise decision. I know how much the store means to you and it meant the same thing to me. Be sure and give my papers to the new owner to help them manage our system. It's only five pages, but those pages represent our lifetime work.

Last of all, you might have some sorrow in giving up the store. Don't, honey. You might have some regrets about our lives together. Don't. I've had the most wonderful life with you. The joy in your heart is contagious. Share it with others. I wanted this letter to be a hidden treasure for you to find, but I don't want you to keep this one. I want you to share it with the new owner so they'll know how much this place has meant to both of us.

I'll see you before you know it.

Love,

Martha

I wiped a tear from my eye. This letter was a precious gift to pass along. Martha was truly a wonderful woman. I could see why Fred missed her so. She called the letter a "Hidden Treasure." I smiled and knew that Martha had just named the store. I knew Fred would love the idea, too. After all, that's what people came in here looking for: Hidden Treasures! Yes! I loved it!

I looked through the five pages and realized it was what FlyLady called a "Student Control Journal" that had been modified for the business. It told exactly how Martha had organized the front of the store and exactly how she ran the day-to-day operations. Most of what was in there Fred had already told me. From having already read the diary, I could clearly see Gina's and especially FlyLady's influence in her life. I immediately added everything to my Control Journal.

I closed everything up that night, but before I left that day, I set FlyLady's book to the side of my desk and set the diary down in the center of the desk. I opened it up to Gina's last entry and picked up a pen and wrote:

> "Gina's journey in this diary was a great help to me. Gina and Susan really had the same mentor as me: FlyLady. FlyLady had her own journey that resulted in Sink Reflections. For whatever it's worth, as you read their journey, know that I took one of my own. Though our destinations were different, the steps were exactly the same. Take those same Baby Steps that FlyLady taught us to do and you will find your purpose, too. Don't worry about feeling like you're behind. Don't try to be perfect. Just jump in where you are and start your own adventure.
>
> "As you read this I hope you learn as much and grow as much as I have. Even though our paths are different, our goal is the same: 'To find joy in all that I do.' I have found my purpose. I know you'll find yours, too.
>
> "I'm SO proud of you!
>
> --- Courtney, Owner and Proprietor, Hidden Treasures"

Epilogue

It's been a year since Fred and Gina left the store. They still come by and see things every now and then. Gina even brought Susan in one time. Although not at all like I had pictured her in my mind, she was an impressive woman. As a matter of fact, Fred and Gina are coming by today to see what I've done with the store.

The business has really exploded. I've been able to create systems for this business just like my home. I've found these systems are applicable to lots of things in my life. I've been able to hire several other people to help. My daughter is working here after school and has become quite the organizer herself.

Speaking of my kids, they have really latched onto the FlyLady concepts and have stepped up to help at home. It makes working here so much easier when everybody pulls their own weight at home.

The place was so synonymous with Fred that most people didn't even know it had a name. It was called "Antiques and More." They just called it "Fred's Junk Store." I like the new name of the store, "Hidden Treasures." It seems to attract a different clientele in addition to the regulars.

I was working in the afternoon when a family walked in. The husband had a frown on his face and a look of disgust as he looked around the room. This was not his cup of tea. They had a boy around 10 who immediately exclaimed, "No toys! Booorrrring!!"

The daughter looked to be around 14 and said, "Mommmmmmm" in that long, drawn out tone only a teenager can do. You could tell the mother was the only one who wanted to be there. She was wearing sweatpants and a non-matching sweatshirt with something resembling a hair clip stuck in her hair that was halfway falling down. As she got closer, the stains on her sweatshirt, which was shaped like the country of Italy, became more apparent.

She walked up to me and said, "Yes, I'm looking for the PERFECT desk."

As soon as I heard the word, "perfect" my ears perked up. I knew this word was an elusive illusion. Was she, just like me, hiding behind her perfectionism? Trying to please everyone? So concerned with insignificant details that she missed the majors in life?

I could tell she was committed to her family and was trying to hold everything together, but she obviously needed help. Was this the one? I was snapped back to the moment as she asked again, "Ma'am, do you have any desks?"

Immediately the teenager, with a roll of her eyes, chimed in, "Mom! We don't need any more junk in our house! It's full already!" then looking at me she said, "No offense, lady, but you just have noooo idea." She then proceeded to pull out her cell phone and start texting.

The mom was undaunted. She smiled in an embarrassed way and said, "I'd like to see what you have."

"Sure," I brightly replied. "I think I have one over here."

The lady started walking to the side of the store. I looked at her as she walked away, her daughter texting away in an irritated manner, her husband and son at the front of the store leaning against the door waiting to get out, and I knew.

I reached under the counter, pulled out the diary and the FlyLady book and smiled because I knew this lady was about to get the deal of the century on a desk that was going to change her entire world.

Now it's your turn to pass on the Hidden Treasures.

This book is lovingly dedicated to Marla Cilley, the FlyLady, who works tirelessly to help each of us discover our own "Hidden Treasures." She has forged the way to make it possible for us to find "Peace in all we do." It is her love and dedication that gives us wings to fly, to finally love ourselves, and to pass that love on to others.

The authors

Paddi Newlin earned a B.S degree (in psychology) from Bryan College, and a Masters from Berea Theological Seminary. She is a Certified Professional Life Coach (CPLC), and is currently working toward her doctorate. Paddi has worked with FlyLady and Company since its inception in 1999, but she has known the Flylady—her sister, Marla Cilley—all her life. A resident of Chattanooga, Tenn., she is the mother of three and a proud grandmother of three.

Ken Hartley is a graduate of Union University in Jackson, Tenn., with a B.A. in music and drama. He has served as a Pastor and Counselor for over 25 years. He also has traveled the world performing as professional illusionist in Europe, Asia, and South America, as well as all over the United States (including Las Vegas). Ken makes his home in Chattanooga, Tenn. He and his wife, Stacey, have been married for twenty-three years. They have four children.

Jessica Oliver has worked for Flylady and Company for ten years, but like her mother Paddi, she has been involved with her aunt the Flylady all her life. Jessica is the mother of one, and makes her home in Chattanooga.

Made in the USA
Lexington, KY
19 September 2015